THE BONE PICKER

Sam 'Buzzard' Jones stumbles across a dying cowboy, whose final words set him on a course that will change his life and have repercussions for an entire nation ... In the cauldron that is Bleeding Kansas, he fights for truth, justice and freedom. With a small band of allies Buzzard battles an unknown organisation — never sure who's a friend and who is a foe — and never knowing where the next bullet is coming from.

DEREK RUTHERFORD

◆

THE BONE PICKER

Complete and Unabridged

LINFORD
Leicester

First published in Great Britain in 2010 by
Robert Hale Limited
London

First Linford Edition
published 2012
by arrangement with
Robert Hale Limited
London

The moral right of the author has been asserted

British Library CIP Data

Rutherford, Derek, 1963 –
  The bone picker.- -(Linford western library)
  1. Western stories.
  2. Large type books.
  I. Title II. Series
  823.9′2–dc23

ISBN 978–1–4448–0989–3

Published by
F. A. Thorpe (Publishing)
Anstey, Leicestershire

Set by Words & Graphics Ltd.
Anstey, Leicestershire
Printed and bound in Great Britain by
T. J. International Ltd., Padstow, Cornwall

This book is printed on acid-free paper

1

Kansas Territory, Summer, 1855

The man was hanging from a tree by his wrists. His feet were three feet from the ground and the dirt beneath him was dark with blood. A jacket and hat lay next to the remnants of a small fire.

'Whoah.'

Buzzard Jones pulled his horse to a halt fifteen yards from the man, and carefully looked around. The sycamore was one of several growing in the lee of a hill; strong trees were a rarity in this region of eastern Kansas. Further along the canyon a group of willows thrived, too. A dry gully ran along the base of the slope. There'd be water here in winter and spring. Enough to make the trees and grass flourish. Tough bushes sprouted in small groups between the trees. Water all year round and it would have made a fine place to build a cabin, sheltered from the wind and the dust.

Buzzard tapped the horse's flanks and eased her forward, twisting in his seat, looking up at the skyline, scanning the rocks. The only movement came from two birds high in the cloudless sky, circling, waiting for him to move on so they could come down and start feeding.

The hanging man's head lolled to one side. The part of his face that Buzzard could see looked raw — either beaten or burned.

Five yards away, Buzzard climbed off the horse.

'Someone didn't care for you much, did they?' he said, walking slowly around the man. Up on the plains the wind would have given the man some movement, pushing him this way and that until he might have almost looked alive. Down here he was as still as the rocks.

Buzzard lifted the man's jacket. It was torn and there was blood on the inside. The pockets were empty. He threw the jacket back down. The man's hat was better. A little sweat stained, but Buzzard would get a price for it.

He looked back at the man. His boots were good, too. Better than good. Wine-coloured, lots of fancy stitching. Plenty of dollars potential there. But when Buzzard gripped the man's leg and pulled on one of his boots the man let out a long low moan that sounded like the noise a fellow might make as he died and realized the Devil himself was waiting.

Buzzard jumped back in surprise, caught his foot in the man's jacket and fell over.

The man said, 'Help me. Help me, please.'

'Mercy,' Buzzard said and scrabbled backwards.

'Help me.'

Buzzard stood up.

'I thought you were dead.'

The man didn't appear to hear. Buzzard stepped closer to him, leaning down to get a better view of the man's face.

'Mercy,' he said again, quietly this time. The man's eyes were gone. Cut out leaving just dark holes in his face. 'Who did this to you?' It looked like Indian work, or at least the sort of thing that Buzzard imagined might be Indian work. But as far as he knew there weren't any savages around these parts — hadn't been for a few years. Anyway, the man still had his hair. Indians would surely have scalped him too.

'Water,' the man said.

'Hold on,' Buzzard said. 'Hold on, fellow.'

Buzzard whistled between his teeth and his horse walked forwards. Buzzard reached into a satchel and pulled out a knife.

He climbed back on to the horse and urged her alongside the man. Then he stood in his stirrups, reached across, and sawed through the rope.

The man fell to the floor and the air expelled from his lungs when he hit the

4

ground sounded like a pig squealing.

''Pologies,' Buzzard said, jumping to the ground again. He slipped the knife back into the bag and pulled a water skin from the rear of his saddle. 'Here.'

He knelt beside the man, lifted his head gently and poured water into the man's bloodied mouth.

The man coughed and gasped. When Buzzard felt him pressing backwards, he lowered the man's head to the ground.

'Who was it?' Buzzard said. 'Who are you?'

'Southerners,' the man said.

'Southerners did this?'

The man's head moved. It may have been a nod or it may have just been an attempt to ease the pain.

'Why?'

'Listen . . . '

Buzzard listened. He couldn't hear anything except the rasp of the man's breathing.

'My name is . . . Curry,' the man said.

Curry. Should he recognize the name? He couldn't place the man, leastways, not with the ruined face.

'Listen . . . '

The man paused again. His breathing stopped and for a moment Buzzard thought he was dead. In a way that would be for the best, he thought.

'There's . . . a family,' Curry said.

'A family?'

'Please . . . More water.'

Buzzard helped him drink again. After Curry had coughed up almost all of the water, much of it mixed with blood, he said, 'Can I trust you?'

'Most people don't,' Buzzard said, a brief flame of anger lighting inside him. 'They say I'm a thief and a vulture. A bone picker. But all I do . . . I just clear up after the dead. Take stuff that they don't need any more and sell it on to those that do.'

Curry was quiet for several seconds Then he said, 'I think I know you. You an abolitionist?' He twisted his head, turning his tortured face towards Buzzard.

'No,' Buzzard said honestly. 'But

6

neither am I in favour. I don't pay much heed — '

'You should.'

'I figure — '

'There's a family,' Curry said. 'Coming over from Missouri. Friday.'

'I should get you into town,' Buzzard said.

'They're going to be hiding out at South Bottom Crossing. Midnight Friday. They need to be taken up to Romego. The stables at Romego. Man there named Powder will do the rest.'

'I don't know why you're telling me this. I — '

'Look at what they did to me.'

'I know, it's — '

'It's nothing to what they're doing to people in Missouri.'

'What do you mean?'

'I mean . . . Please, water.'

Buzzard gave Curry more water. This time he coughed up what looked like blood with a little water added, rather than the other way around.

'Let me get you to town,' Buzzard

said. 'Sawbones — '

'This family are . . . witnesses. They will stand before the Senate and tell what they've seen.'

Curry started coughing again. Buzzard felt flecks of phlegm splatter his face.

'You'll help them,' Curry said, his face pointing upwards.

Buzzard looked away.

'You'll help them,' Curry said again.

'You're talking about slaves?'

'Yes.'

'Nobody'll believe what slaves say.'

'These they will.'

'Why?'

Curry started coughing again. Now it was pure blood spraying from his mouth. His empty eye sockets screwed up in pain. When the coughing stopped he fought to get breath into his lungs.

'Why?' Buzzard asked.

'They did this to set an example,' Curry said eventually. 'To scare people off. You're not scared, are you? Just don't trust — '

More coughing.

Buzzard ran a hand over one of his own cheeks. It came away smeared with Curry's blood.

'What's so special about these slaves?' he said. 'Who shouldn't I trust?'

Curry opened his mouth to speak but started choking again. His lungs were full of blood and Buzzard had to roll him on to his side to let the blood out and the oxygen in. He wondered if he had inadvertently caused this damage when he'd cut Curry down, or maybe even by giving him so much water. But that was nonsense, the man's clothes were covered in blood. It looked like he'd been stabbed and shot *and* burned. The Southerners, whoever they were, were well and truly to blame.

'Curry,' he said, when the man's retching had stopped. 'Who shouldn't I trust?'

The man never said anything.

'Curry?'

The man was still, too still. Buzzard rolled him back over. Every time he'd seen dead people before he knew they were dead because of their eyes. Eyes that were open but not seeing, open and unfocused, open and cloudy.

He wasn't sure how to tell if someone with no eyes was dead, so he just sat there a while, hunched over on his ankles looking at the blood that seemed to be everywhere. He looked at Curry's face and he thought of men who could do such things to a fellow human being. He thought of slaves and he pictured the river at South Bottom Crossing and how far it was from there to Romego. He figured it was a crazy man who'd get involved in such things when clearly there were very good reasons — mostly about retaining one's eyesight — not to. Then he thought about how this man had trusted him. About how Curry hadn't even seen him, just *listened* to him, to Buzzard's own self-deprecating mini biography, and had made a decision to trust a person whom most people saw as being barely one step up from the town's rubbish-dump rats.

Later, he took a long drink of water, stood up and walked back to his horse. He climbed up and was about to ride on. He paused, jumped down again, and went over to Curry's body.

'Forgive me,' he said, and pulled Curry's fine boots from his feet.

2

The boy, Frankie Meyer, who was just six years old, handed Mary Colton the envelope and said, 'That fellow there said for me to give you this, miss.'

Mary looked down the dusty street to where Frankie was pointing. There wasn't much to look at. Molloy's saloon and the mercantile, Kasey's bunkhouse, the livery, and beyond that the wooden framework of several new buildings in various stages of completion, and a veritable city of dirty-white tents where the people putting up those buildings were currently living. Some ambitious person was even laying stone foundations for something, and there were dozens of carts piled high with brown bricks. After that it was just dirt and dust all the way to where the ground rose up and turned a little green way off in the distance.

'I guess he's gone,' Frankie said.

'Who was he?'

The envelope was smudged with dirt. Mary couldn't think of anyone she knew — or would like to know — who'd send her a letter covered in grease and finger-marks.

'I ain't never seen him before,' Frankie said. 'But he told me you'd give me a bit for delivery.'

'Did he, indeed?'

'Yeah.' Frankie smiled.

'Well, next time you see him you tell him that the sender pays.'

'You ain't going to pay me?'

She looked down at him. She'd only been running the tiny schoolroom for a few months and Frankie had only just started turning up, but already he was amongst the cheekiest and funniest boys there.

'This time,' she said. 'But you make sure you tell him next time.'

Frankie grinned as she opened her purse and dropped a coin into his hand. 'You think he likes you, miss?'

'Frankie!'

'He was good looking.'

'Was he?'

'He was tall and had a beard, miss. Though he only had one arm.'

'Frankie!'

'No, I mean it, miss. I've never seen a man with just one arm before.'

She couldn't recall knowing such a man either.

'OK, thanks Frankie.'

She opened the letter, standing there on the main street of New Whitby, with a faint — and almost permanent — taste of dust in her mouth and the warm wind on her skin.

After she'd read the few words, she looked up and down the street, her breathing faster now, her heart-beat heavier. There was no sign of any tall handsome man with a beard and just one arm. But was he out there, watching her, seeing how she'd react?

She read the note again. Then she folded it up, slipped it inside her purse, and hurried off towards the church.

'It's a trap,' Father Wiseman said.

'I don't think so,' Mary Colton said. 'They don't need to set traps. I heard they dragged people out of their beds in the Topeka hotel. It's . . . outrageous.'

'I heard about it, too. But Whitby is not Topeka, Mary.'

'Are they trying to frighten us into giving up?' she said.

'I would imagine so.'

Mary watched Father Wiseman read the note again. *A friend of yours and a friend of slaves is hanging at Willow Canyon.*

'Who is it?' Mary said. 'Who have they got?' She could hear the fear in her own voice.

'When did you get this? Ten minutes ago? You said someone gave it to one of the boys to give you and that he'd never seen the man before.'

She nodded.

'Ten minutes.' He thought for a moment. 'I saw Lloyd Avery not half an

15

hour ago heading towards his office.'

'So it's either Luther or John then.' Mary paused, then added, 'Unless it's someone new. Somebody from the North they picked at random.'

Wiseman shook his head. 'They were very specific in delivering it to you. There are far more . . . open organizations than ours. This isn't random.'

'Then they know about us.'

'We have to assume so.'

She took the note from his hand. 'If they've killed Luther or John then what's to stop them killing all of us?' She looked up at him. He always seemed so wise and calm, the thick grey beard and the piercing blue eyes somehow giving him a saintly aura. It was what had drawn her to him when she'd first met him. That, and what he was trying to do for his fellow men, whatever their colour. Maybe, she thought, he'd seen something similar in her, coming from the East, enlightened, determined to do something good for the children of the West and not afraid

16

to debate the rights and wrongs — mostly wrongs — of slavery. She remembered getting into similar debates with Lloyd Avery, a man trying desperately to get a newspaper up and running in New Whitby, and some time later being delighted when Lloyd had suggested there might be someone she'd like to meet if she was interested in acting on her feeling, and the man turning out to be Father Wiseman. There were others, too, John Cowmeadow, who ran a ranch-cum-farm several miles outside of town, and Luther Curry, a businessman from the East. Though she was also well aware that theirs was but one small part of a much greater machine, and there were no doubt many more people involved.

'Of course, maybe they don't know how many of us there are,' Wiseman said.

'They'd laugh if they knew.'

'Mary, for what we do, small is better.'

'They obviously know me,' she said, a little ashamed of the fear she felt.

'Yes.' He went to say something else, stopped, and instead cast his eyes heavenwards. Then he looked at the large wooden crucifix at the front of the small church.

'Yes, what?' Mary said. 'You were about to say something else.'

'Maybe it is time you stopped. This last few months it's become far more dangerous.'

'I'm not stopping now. Luther said . . . '

'Luther said what?'

'He said the next ones would be *the* ones.'

'*The* ones. Yes. What do you think he meant?'

'I don't know. Something big, I assumed. Something that would make a difference.'

'If it's Luther' — Wiseman nodded towards the note — 'we may have to rebuild contacts on the Missouri side. Luther was the one they knew. The one they trusted. Maybe it is time to stop and rethink.'

She looked at the note, and felt determination overpowering the fear within her. 'We should go. I know where Willow Canyon is.'

'It's too dangerous.'

'Father, it might be — '

'I'll send someone. I'll send a dozen. Good men, too. If it's a trap then whoever did this had better have a God to pray too, as well.'

* * *

'In the money, Buzzard?' Sheldon Molloy said, smiling. 'Found a dead person to rob, did you?'

Molloy's saloon was almost empty. There was a fellow sat close to the window reading the latest — and so far, only the second — issue of Lloyd Avery's *Sentinel* and a couple more playing cards in a darker corner over by the piano. The counter ran three-quarters of the way along the wall opposite the window. There were three mirrors on the wooden wall behind the counter, mirrors that Molloy had long since given up trying to keep clean, and, on the shelves between the mirrors, bottles and glasses. On a long table beneath the mirrors Molloy had several large barrels of ale which he brewed himself out back.

The afternoon light shone through the windows, reflected in the mirrors, and gave the room a bright and open feel. Come nightfall, Molloy would pull curtains across the windows and light a dozen oil lanterns. One time a drunken rider had knocked an oil lamp over on to the dirt floor. Most of the burning oil had soaked into the floor, but some of the spillage had reached the counter, which had caught alight. A quick-thinking cowboy had thrown his beer over the burning wood and the fire had died. The scorch marks still remained, as did the consensus that Molloy's beer couldn't contain much alcohol or surely the fire would have taken greater hold.

Buzzard pushed forward the coins he'd laid down on the counter.

'My money's as good as anyone's.'

'I was only joking, Buzz. God knows, if you weren't here I'd be the butt of all the jokes.'

Buzzard grunted. He wasn't in the mood for the snide comments that people in Whitby generally made about his line of work. Hell, there were folks all around the territory with new saddles and waterproof slickers, bed-rolls and tobacco pouches, coils of rope and blankets because of him. Folks with guns and knives and even wagons and horses that they'd got through deals he'd brokered. Most times, he was the middle man, taking the pain and hard work out of disposing of a loved one's possessions and passing the proceeds — minus his commission — right back to where it was due. It was harder than winter to obtain anything out here so he was doing a service to the living just as much as the dead. Yet even so most people still seemed to see him as little more than a common thief. Sure, there were the occasional days, like this morning, when fate would see him pick something up from which he could take *all* the profit. But such days were rare.

He raised the shot-glass that Molloy placed in front of him, paused briefly, his mind on the man called Curry, then downed the drink in one. The whiskey burned his throat and made his eyes water.

He said, 'Another one please, Moll.'

'You all right?' Molloy said.

'I'll risk a beer, too.'

'Celebrating or commiserating?'

'Neither.'

'Just thirsty, huh?'

Molloy placed a glass of cloudy beer on the counter, then pulled a cork from a whiskey bottle and refilled Buzzard's shot-glass.

'You ever wonder what it would be like to be blind?' Buzzard said.

'Blind?'

'Yeah, blind. You know, no eyes.'

The man reading the paper by the window looked up and said, 'You drink enough of Molloy's whiskey and you're liable to find out.'

'My whiskey's guaranteed, Jasper.' Molloy said.

'Guaranteed to rot the gut,' the man called Jasper said. 'I still recall that batch of Mexican you brought in a while back.'

'That wasn't my fault,' Molloy said. 'Anyway, those guys were looking for a fight. It wasn't nothing to do with my whiskey.'

'So why d'you sell it on so cheaply to those traders heading West? That stuff made men meaner'n snakes. I seem to recall Plymouth King — and Buzzard here — were busy that week.'

Buzzard took a long draught of beer. It was true, there'd been a lot of fighting that week, most of it over nothing, and four men had found themselves on the wrong end of bullets. After that, Plymouth started joking that his cemetery — up on the rise, north of town — was the most populated plot in all of New Whitby. And he was probably right.

'So what's this about being blind?' Jasper said. 'You're not losing your sight, are you?'

'No,' he said. 'Something just got me thinking, that's all.'

'What something?' Molloy asked.

Buzzard sank the second whiskey. He didn't want to talk to them about Curry. He still didn't feel good about what he'd done. It wasn't the taking of the man's boots — hell, he'd done that often enough in the past. It was the taking of them after the conversation they'd had. The man had been killed — tortured — because of his beliefs. Buzzard couldn't imagine possessing such a commitment. Stealing a fellow like that's footwear seemed wrong, plain cowardly almost. That was the other thing. Curry had asked him to do something and there was no way in the world, not for all the silver dollars in the territories, that he was going to do it. And *that* really did feel cowardly. Curry had gone through so much and right at the end had asked a stranger something

— no, had *trusted* a stranger with something — and that stranger wasn't interested.

'I heard tell some Indians had staked a man out,' Buzzard said. 'And cut his eyelids off.'

'Not round these parts,' Molloy said. 'The Indians round here are all friendly drunks.'

'Least until they drink some of Molloy's whiskey,' Jasper said.

'I just got to thinking about it,' Buzzard said. 'And couldn't stop.'

'Yeah, some things get you like that,' Molloy said. 'More whiskey?'

★　★　★

A dozen men brought Luther Curry in that evening, his body laid on the back of a flat wagon and covered with a tarp. They hauled up outside the sheriff's office, but when one of them went inside the sheriff wasn't there. A crowd started to gather outside, wanting to know who it was and what had happened, but the men who'd ridden out to Willow Canyon refused to remove the tarp.

'He's dead, and that's all that matters,' one of the riders said.

'Who is it?' someone cried.

'We think it's Luther Curry.'

'*Think*,' somebody else said. 'Why only think? Let me see. I know Luther.'

'He's been cut up and burned,' another rider said.

'Luther Curry,' a woman whispered. 'He's one of the abolitionists.'

'*Was* one of 'em,' somebody corrected.

One of the riders went and called on Plymouth King, the undertaker. By the time he wandered down to the wagon the crowd was more than thirty in size. Several people were arguing, some were saying that Luther had gotten exactly what he deserved and he was a fool to stick up for slaves, whilst others insisted that it was attitudes like that which would see the country forever stay in the

Dark Ages. A few put it more bluntly — insulting each other, spitting on the floor and even on each other's boots. Somebody called someone else's mother an ugly pig. A punch was thrown. Two men started grappling, One hooked his foot behind the other's knee and they fell to the floor. A woman tried to prise the top one off. Another man grabbed her.

'Leave 'em be, miss.'

The woman's husband pushed the man in the chest. 'You take your hands off my wife.'

The man punched the husband on the chin. The wife screamed and started flailing at the man's face. The man punched her and she went down. Someone else took exception to a woman being hit and he lashed out. Within seconds there were a dozen people fighting.

A shot rang out.

Everybody stopped.

Plymouth King was kneeling on the back of the wagon, a smoking gun in his hand, the barrel pointing skyward.

'Have some respect,' he said. 'There's a dead man here.'

Up and down the street doors opened and curtains moved at the sound of the gunshot.

'Is it Luther?' someone asked.

Plymouth looked down at the tarpaulin.

'You might want to leave him covered,' one of the riders said.

'They need to see what they're becoming,' Plymouth said, and pulled back the canvas.

Further down Main Street — the only street — leaning on the new railing outside Molloy's, Buzzard Jones watched the commotion. He saw Plymouth fire his gun into the air and he saw most people stop fighting. One fellow got in a couple of cheap shots on the man he'd been grappling with but then he too eased off. A moment later a few people seemed to jump back from the wagon in horror, others pressed forward.

Buzzard figured he wasn't going to be the only one having nightmares tonight about getting one's eyes gouged out.

3

The next morning, Thursday, Plymouth King knocked on Buzzard's door at Kasey Christchurch's Bunkhouse. Kasey had already made Plymouth a cup of coffee, and when Buzzard opened the door, his head aching from all the whiskey he'd put down the night before, his face feeling dry and gritty, and his mouth tasting like he'd fallen down on the way home and landed face first in a pile of horseshit, Plymouth was standing there, perfectly turned out in his vest and jacket and shiny shoes, a gold watch chain running from a buttonhole into his vest pocket, the coffee — in a cup and saucer — in his hand.

'Figured I'd give you first shot at making some money,' Plymouth said. 'The way I always do.'

Plymouth wore a pair of round wire spectacles and had a beard but no moustache. Buzzard had no idea how old the man was. Maybe even as much as forty.

'You get your share,' Buzzard said. He ran a hand down his face and sighed.

'A man has to make a living.'

'You do pretty well.'

'A little grouchy, are we this morning? Spend a little too much at Mr Molloy's?'

'I had a drink.'

'Look at this place,' Plymouth said. He glanced around the small room. 'You could do a lot better if you saved a little money, or at least spent it on something other than whiskey.'

'It's what I do. It's what's expected of me.'

Plymouth looked at him, then wandered over to the window — it took just three steps — and pulled open the thin curtains.

'Daylight,' he said.

'Is it the fellow they brought in last night?'

'Uh-huh. An abolitionist by the name

of Luther Curry.'

'I know him.'

'You do?'

'You think Kasey will make me one of those?'

'Not until you put some pants on. How do you know Curry?'

'I know of him. Transportation and distribution.'

'Transportation and distribution, I'm impressed.'

'People think I'm just a drunk who steals off the dead,' Buzzard said.

'I don't think that.'

'Not you. I always make sure a man's belongings go to the right people. Or at least the money from those belongings. That means asking a lot of questions. Talking to people.'

'And you've talked to Curry?'

Buzzard nodded. He looked around the room, found his trousers under the iron bed, and sat on the soft mattress whilst he worked his way into them.

The truth was that Buzzard had never spoken to Luther Curry before yesterday morning. He'd been riding back from Herb Jordan's ranch way out on the McCullough Trail where he'd spent two days relaxing, celebrating July the fourth, and catching up with Herb when he'd come across Curry. After he'd had a few drinks in Molloy's in the afternoon to calm his nerves he'd asked a few contacts around town if they knew the man. He hadn't really been sure what he'd been trying to learn — only that he still felt guilty, and not a little cowardly about his lack of intention regarding the man's final request. It turned out the man arranged for goods from the East to be brought in to New Whitby's growing legion of stores and businesses and building projects. He was a middleman, Buzzard thought. Just like me.

'You should know he died hard,' Plymouth said.

'I heard.'

'You're always ahead of me.'

'Contacts,' Buzzard said, easing his boots on.

'You know where he lived?'

'No.'

'I'm one on up on you there, then.'

Buzzard stood up, slipped a shirt on over his stained undershirt and said, 'Let's go and get me a coffee.'

* * *

'You don't waste any time, do you?' Luther Curry's landlady, Jessica Day, said.

Buzzard smiled. Kasey's rooms might have been smaller than Jessica's. Her mattresses might have been thinner and her lodgers poorer, but she was sweet and pretty, and she cared for her men like they were her own kin. Even before he'd asked she'd had a hot brew waiting for him that morning. Jessica Day was fifteen years older than Kasey, had skin dryer than a rattlesnake's and a meaner reputation, too.

'Just doing my job,' he said.

'What happened to Luther?'

For a moment he thought about telling her the truth, see if he could crack that hard face. 'I heard he ran into a gang up at Willow Creek. They shot him and stole what they could.'

'I bet it was some of those new folks from the North,' she said. 'Half of them haven't got work. They've brought them in just to rig the voting.'

Jessica wasn't wrong. The abolitionists were shipping in Northern folk just as the pro-slavery brigade were bringing in people from the slave states. Sometimes it felt as though Whitby — and Kansas — was a vacuum into which people were being sucked, and once in it, they were getting spun round and round until they crashed into each other. It meant a lot of work for people like him and Plymouth, and a lot of opportunities for folks like Luther Curry, too. He wondered who had paid to put up Jessica Day's guest-house. Someone had invested in it and would be making money day in, day out. Maybe Jessica herself. She looked as though she could build a house single-handedly.

'I don't know who it was,' Buzzard said.

'Well I doubt the sheriff will find out, either. All he does is walk around town getting free drinks and food from anyone he can and then sleeps it all off somewhere. Where was he yesterday when all that fighting was happening?'

'I don't know.'

'That was those Northern folk, you know.'

'May I see Luther's room?'

Jessica sighed. 'Yes, of course. Follow me. You do know he has no family here? I don't mean *here*.' She waved a hand in the vague direction of the door. 'I mean Whitby. Who does have family in Whitby?'

'I understand.'

'But I believe he has a wife back East.'

She paused at the bottom of some narrow stairs.

'Tell me, what's a man doing out here if he has a wife back home? A man should be with his wife, don't you think?'

Depends what the wife's like, Buzzard thought, resisting the urge to ask Jessica if she'd ever considered taking a husband.

'Sometimes a man has to travel to make his fortune,' he said. 'To make a better life for those back home.'

She looked at him with a touch of surprise in her eyes as if she hadn't expected anything remotely profound or touching to escape from his lips.

There was little of value in the room. Some clothes and a Bible, a nice pen and ink set and several books full of details on stocks, orders, and deliveries, customer names and accounts and, in one, a long list of deposits he'd made at the Liberty County Bank over in Missouri.

Tucked into the back of one book was a photograph of a handsome dark haired girl. Buzzard looked at it for a long time. It still amazed him how they could do such things. It was magic, he thought. The girl's name was Bella. It was written on the back page of the book. Along with her address.

★ ★ ★

He was sitting at the bureau in Kasey's parlour, trying to compose a letter, when the schoolteacher walked in.

It was always hard knowing what to say and how to write it. Not the actual mechanics of writing — most folks, Plymouth and Kasey aside, had no idea that Buzzard could read and write — but the message itself. He wanted to let Bella know what had happened, to express his sorrow, and to apologize for making some decisions without reference to her. He was sending her the pen set and the Bible and the journals, but he'd taken the liberty of selling Luther's few clothes (he'd sold Luther's boots the day before to Rodney Purse down at the Mercantile. Rodney would no doubt sell them on. The money he'd made yesterday — some of which he'd drunk — would all be made up and included in the delivery) and was sending her the proceeds, minus a very small commission. But it wasn't enough.

He wanted to tell her more, something about how Luther had been so determined to make the world a better place for those people enslaved by others that he had been killed for his beliefs. He wanted to get across something of Luther's bravery without upsetting Bella with details of what had actually happened. But it was hard. Buzzard felt that he didn't know enough about Luther Curry or his beliefs and convictions to do the man justice. And he desperately wanted to do so. Maybe because he'd been with the man in his last terrible moments. Or maybe because he simply wanted to do *something* right by the man.

'Buzzard Jones,' Mary Colton said. 'With a pen in his hand.'

He looked round.

'I'm just pretending,' he said. 'Pretending I was in your class, miss.'

She was young and pretty. Short blonde hair that had been darker, longer and more curly when she'd first arrived but, like her skin, which was now a little drier and more sunburnt, the Kansas sun and wind had already taken their toll. He found himself wondering who cut her hair? He couldn't imagine her down at the barber's tent. Maybe she did it herself. Nevertheless, she was still just about the nicest looking girl in town, and Buzzard felt as though he was experiencing a ray of sunshine on a cold day.

'Heaven forbid,' she said.

He stood up. 'Can I get you something? A drink?'

'Kasey's already asked,' she said. 'I'm OK.'

'Maybe I'll get a coffee.'

'What are you writing?'

'A letter. To Bella Curry.'

Mary raised her eyebrows.

'Luther Curry's widow,' Buzzard said.

'I know. Well, I know now. Until a few minutes ago I didn't know he was married,' she said. 'Jessica Day told me. Luther always was secretive.'

'You knew him?'

'It's why I'm here. I went over to his

39

room and Jessica said you'd already been there. She said you didn't waste any time moving in on the dead.'

'Sounds like Jessica.'

'She said as far as she knew he never had much in the way of possessions, but what he did have you're sending back East.'

'Some of it is worth more here than there,' Buzzard said. 'I'll sell some and send Bella the proceeds.' He looked at Mary Colton, never realizing until right then how grey her eyes were. Pretty grey. Eyes that could make a man become careless. He thought of Luther Curry's last words: *Just don't trust . . . .* And he looked away from those pretty eyes. Was she the one he shouldn't trust? Why else was she here?

'Can I see what you've got?' she said.

'Let me get that coffee,' he said. 'You sure you won't have one?'

'No, thank you.'

He walked through into Kasey's kitchen. Kasey was standing over the stove. She smiled and raised an eyebrow. Another good-looking woman, he thought. Older than Mary Colton, maybe even older than me. He'd never enquired about her age, and anyway, he wasn't wholly sure about his own. Kasey was a redhead, who, in another place — Chicago, maybe — could have been spectacular. But out here the sun and the dust and the wind seemed to draw the colour out of people.

'Kasey,' he said. 'It's not what you — '

'You have nice writing,' Mary said from the parlour. There was surprise in her voice.

When she came into the kitchen Buzzard said, 'Luther had a nice pen set. I'm tempted to buy it off myself, so to speak, and send Bella the money. But it may have sentimental value. Other than that there was just a Bible, some clothes I'll sell here, and all his accounts. I've already sold his boots.'

'Accounts?' Mary asked.

'Just a list of what he paid for things from suppliers and what he sold them for here.'

41

'That's it?'

'Is there something specific you're after? Some specific reason you're after it?'

She looked at him, smiled, flashed her pretty grey eyes. He felt that urge to be careless coming on.

'No.' Mary sighed. She looked at Kasey, as if to include her in the conversation. 'Well, maybe. I don't know.'

'I don't mean this to sound rude,' Buzzard said. 'But you're not making much sense.'

'It's difficult.'

'I may be sharper than I look.'

'Sorry, I didn't mean to sound . . . patronizing.' She emphasized the last word as if unsure whether it would be too difficult for him, as if she was teaching her kids a new word.

'It's OK,' he said. 'I know what patronizing means.'

'Oh dear.' She bit her bottom lip with her top teeth. Buzzard felt a shudder sweep through his shoulders. He tried to hide it. He didn't know whether Mary had noticed but he knew Kasey would have. 'Even me using that word came out sounding — '

'It's OK. Now, what's so difficult?'

She looked around the kitchen, smiled at Kasey, cocked her head to one side as if listening for something. The movement exaggerated the smooth line of her neck.

'Shall we take a walk?' she said.

He sipped the strong, hot coffee, then put the cup down on the table.

'Sure.'

Outside she said, 'Tell me where you stand on emancipation, Mr Jones.'

He looked across and down the street to where Molloy's swing doors beckoned. A dog was curled up on the plank walk, asleep in the sun. Several saddled horses were hitched to the railing outside. Further along was the sheriff's office, where only last night good folk had been fighting each other over the rights of black people. It was no secret that Luther Curry had been mixed up in the battle to influence, if not directly steer, Kansas's position on slavery. A couple of covered wagons being pulled by teams of mules that appeared to be on their last legs driven by men who didn't look as though they'd be far behind, trundled past.

'I think it's wrong that folk are being herded into the territory like cattle,' he said, 'Just to vote one way or the other. In the end the legislation will be about which side managed to mobilize the most people — the North, or the South. What about the people who live here? I mean, who really live here? The ones that came here before all this. Their voice will be lost.'

'You're one of those people,' she said. She slipped her hand through his arm as they walked. He could smell soap and perfume on her.

'Are you trying to influence my answer?'

She smiled.

'Just two friends out for a walk,' she said.

'You'll get a bad reputation walking with me.'

'I've got a bad reputation, anyway.'

'You have?' He looked at her.

'Well, with half the town anyway. Half the *activists*.'

'I guess I know where your allegiance lies,' he said. 'On account of you asking about Mr Curry.'

Just don't trust . . .

'And you? You haven't answered my question.'

'No.'

'Well?'

'I keep my own counsel.'

For a moment he thought she was about to slide her arm from his, step away from him, get angry with him.

'You're on their side, aren't you?'

'I never said that.'

'It's inhumane,' she said. 'All these people . . . they purport to be religious, yet . . . Why are you smiling?'

'You're making assumptions about me.'

'Well, if you're too cowardly to stand

up and state your position.'

She smiled at someone she knew, maybe a parent of one of her pupils, he thought. Her arm was still through his, her smile and her eyes were still both bright, yet her words seemed carefully chosen to cut into him.

'You know nothing about me,' he said.

'What does that mean?'

'Maybe my priorities are different from yours.'

They stopped. Before them the plank walk ended, unfinished. The dust at ground level looked alive, thousands of tiny swirls moving around in a light breeze that felt warm and sleep-inducing in his face.

'There is no bigger priority than this right now,' she said, turning to face him.

'What did you want from Luther Curry's possessions?'

She looked at him and it felt as though her eyes were seeing further inside him than he was comfortable with. She's trying to establish whether or not she can trust me, he thought.

'I don't know,' she said. 'Can I see his books?'

He looked into her grey eyes, nodded, and hoped that he wasn't being careless.

4

'There was nothing,' Mary Colton said.

Father Wiseman nodded. 'To be honest I didn't expect there to be. He kept it all in his head.'

John Cowmeadow, leaning against the doorframe, said, 'Bullshit.' He looked at his companions and slammed the bottom of his fist against one of his huge thighs. 'He never kept *everything* in his head. What's the matter with you people?'

Lloyd Avery sat at a table, a small leather tobacco pouch open in front of him. He was carefully rolling a cigarette.

'He told me,' Lloyd said, 'that as soon as it was all fixed up he'd let me know who and where. Said this time he had to be real careful.'

They were in one of the rooms at the back of the church. Curtains covered the only window and where the sunlight slipped through around the edges dust motes could be seen in several long streams in the air.

John Cowmeadow said, 'I told the son of a bitch he should share.' He sighed loudly. 'There has to be something. He would've had something written down. He was a businessman. You say he wrote everything down about his business?'

'Yes.'

'But nothing about . . . this?'

'Exactly,' Mary said.

'It doesn't add up. You went through it all? His clothes, his pockets.'

'John, I wanted to find something as badly as you did. There was nothing.'

'It was in his head,' Father Wiseman said.

'What about the clothes they found him in?' Lloyd Avery said. He'd finished making one cigarette and was now working on a second. Father Wiseman didn't like anyone smoking in the church room. He said it made his robes smell, said it made his bed in the room next door smell. Said it made him sleep poorly. But there was nothing wrong with taking the opportunity to roll a few.

'I had a word with Plymouth,' Wiseman said. 'He'd been robbed as well as . . . murdered. They took everything, even his boots.'

'Buzzard Jones told me *he*'d sold Luther's boots,' Mary said.

'Maybe Plymouth was mistaken,' Wiseman said.

'Maybe Buzzard was lying,' Cowmeadow said, pushing himself away from the doorframe.

'What reason would he have for lying?' Lloyd Avery said.

'Buzzard's only interested in money,' Mary said.

Cowmeadow said. 'Maybe he found something. One of my horsemen, Raul, came all the way from Mexico with five silver dollars in the hollowed-out heel of his boot.'

Lloyd said, 'What are the odds of

that, John? A hollowed-out heel.'

'What are you saying? That you want to ignore it?'

'I'm just saying what are the odds that Luther had — '

'I told the story to Luther,' Cowmeadow said. 'One time when we were just talking. Maybe I sowed the seeds.'

'Buzzard's a good man,' Mary said. 'An *honest* man, at least.'

Cowmeadow said, 'All I'm saying is he lied about the boots. Maybe there's something about them. Maybe we should check it out.'

'John — ' Wiseman sighed.

'This was going to be *the* one,' Cowmeadow said.

'You're clutching at straws, John,' Wiseman said. He pressed his fingers into his beard. 'Let's face it, this one may have got away from us.'

'I'm not giving up that easily,' Cowmeadow said. 'This one was going to make the difference.'

'So what do you suggest?' Wiseman asked.

'I suggest we go and ask Buzzard Jones what he found in Luther's boots. Leastways where the boots are now.'

'Maybe we ought to just lie low,' Mary said. 'I mean . . . they — whoever they are — know about us.'

Wiseman looked at Mary and said, 'No one would blame you if — '

'Look,' Avery said. 'Luther's gone. This opportunity might be gone. That's the way it is. We have to rebuild. I agree with Mary. You guys lie low for a while. Tomorrow, after Luther's funeral, I'll head back into Missouri. I can say I'm doing a story for the *Sentinel* — I need paper and ink and some tools anyway. I'll try and find out who Luther was dealing with over there. I've got a name or two.'

'You do that,' Cowmeadow said, snorting, pulling open the door hard enough for the wood to groan. 'I'm going to see Buzzard Jones. Ask him about these boots.'

★ ★ ★

'Seen you out walking with that pretty schoolmarm earlier,' Molloy said.

Buzzard sipped his beer.

'Seems like you lucked out a bit there, fellow.'

Buzzard put his beer down and wiped the back of his hand over his lips.

'We're just friends,' he said, staring at the brew. It looked better than it tasted.

'She looked mighty happy,' Molloy said. 'Can't think why.'

Buzzard looked up. 'A man could get fooled pretty easy by that one.'

'Meaning what?'

'I don't know, Moll. I really don't.'

'You don't seem very happy,' Molloy said. 'Considering.'

Buzzard turned, his back against the bar, his elbows resting on it, and looked round the room. It was late afternoon, too early to be busy, just the usual old timers playing cards and a fellow sat at one of the tables working his way through a bowl of Mrs Molloy's stew, a folded up copy of the *Sentinel* alongside the plate. Outside he saw a couple of strangers ride along Main Street, their heads moving from side to side as if they were looking for something — or someone — in particular. There'd been a lot of strangers around this last month or so. Sometimes he wondered if there weren't entire towns empty of people down South and up North.

'You know, I never planned on staying here this long,' Buzzard said.

'You mean in my saloon or in Whitby?'

'I mean Whitby.'

'You leave, my profits will tumble.'

'I'm not leaving. That's my point. Things have worked out well for me here.'

'So why the worried look? You're making money and this morning you had the prettiest girl in town on your arm.'

Buzzard drank more beer.

'I don't know,' he said. 'I just have a feeling it's all about to go wrong.'

The light changed in the bar as the swing doors opened and someone came in. Buzzard looked round. He vaguely recognized the new man, had seen him around town once or twice, but couldn't really place him. The man was tall, with wide shoulders. He was heavy around the chest and stomach. A strong man.

'Figured I'd find you in here,' the man said, striding towards Buzzard.

'Me?' Buzzard said.

'You're Buzzard Jones'

'I am.'

'Then yes. You sold Luther Curry's boots?'

The man was red-faced, either angry or in a hurry.

'Nothing wrong with that,' Buzzard said, purposefully taking his time in answering, granting himself respect even if the big man wasn't prepared to do so. 'It's what I do. Mr Curry's widow will be getting — '

'Who d'you sell 'em to? What was in 'em?'

'Hold up,' Buzzard said. 'What is this? Who are you?'

'John Cowmeadow,' Molloy interrupted. 'Can I get you drink, John?'

Cowmeadow looked at him. 'I'm in a rush.'

'I can tell that,' Molloy said.

'Over a pair of boots?' Buzzard said.

'Yeah, over a pair of boots.'

'They were just boots,' Buzzard said. 'Red ones. Fancy, admittedly, but just boots.'

Cowmeadow glared at him. 'Who'd you sell 'em to?'

'Whoah,' Buzzard said. 'I'm not sure I'm obliged to tell, especially considering I don't know you, or why you're so keen on these boots.'

Buzzard saw Cowmeadow's right hand clench into a fist. Across the room he heard someone say, 'Easy, John.'

'Luther Curry was a good friend of mine.'

Buzzard nodded, but didn't say anything. He stared at John Cowmeadow, saw the redness growing in the man's cheeks; he was a man who clearly wasn't used to not getting his way.

'Beer,' Molloy said, putting a glass on to the counter. 'On the house, John.'

'The boots,' Cowmeadow said.

Buzzard lifted his own glass, slowly finished the drink, put the glass down, and said, 'Mr Cowmeadow, I don't want no trouble. I sold those boots in good faith. It's what I do. The sheriff knows what I do. Plymouth King knows what I do. Luther Curry's landlady knows what I do and his widow will get the proceeds.'

'You're making money off a dead man,' Cowmeadow said. 'You're a — '

'Vulture,' Buzzard said, and smiled. 'A bone picker. But I'm not having my customers bullied by people I don't even know.'

'You're a . . . parasite.'

'That's a new one — '

'And a liar, too,' Cowmeadow said.

'What's this all about, John?' Molloy said.

'Buzzard made sure he got to Luther first,' Cowmeadow said. 'I want to know why.'

'It's what I do,' Buzzard said. 'Plymouth King called me up — '

'You lied about the boots. You said — '

'I don't know what a pair of boots has to do with anything. I do know I don't have to stand here and take being called a liar. Good day, Mr Cowmeadow.'

Buzzard made to walk past Cowmeadow, but Cowmeadow reached out, grabbed Buzzard's right arm above the elbow and crashed him back against the counter.

'You ain't going until you answer my questions about Luther.'

'Let go of my arm.'

Molloy said, 'John, I'm sure Buzzard will tell you anything you want to know if you're just a little bit more civil.'

Buzzard twisted his shoulder backwards to wrench his arm free. His back hurt where Cowmeadow had slammed him against the counter. His biceps hurt where the man's fingers had dug into him.

'Forget it, Moll,' he said. 'I'm not telling this bastard anything.'

He went to step around Cowmeadow again.

Cowmeadow said, 'I told you . . . ' He lunged forward to grab Buzzard's arm again. This time Buzzard stepped sideways and caught Cowmeadow's wrist, pulled it hard and fast in the direction that Cowmeadow was moving, and stuck out his foot. Cowmeadow sprawled to the floor. Buzzard twisted the man's wrist as he fell, holding on to it until the man's weight wrenched it free. Buzzard wasn't sure, but he thought he heard a bone crack.

One of the old-timers laughed.

Molloy said, 'Oh Lord.'

John Cowmeadow growled, 'Son of a bitch' and came up swinging.

The man was too big to be fast. Buzzard danced backwards as the wild punches flashed by in front of his face.

'Listen,' he said, breathlessly, rocking his body to the right to avoid another of Cowmeadow's haymakers. 'I don't know . . . why . . . you're so riled but' — Buzzard threw several punches of his own, short snappy punches that caught Cowmeadow on the nose and in the eye — 'You might want to say please next time.'

Buzzard hit Cowmeadow hard on the chin. He felt the skin on his knuckles split.

Cowmeadow roared and now, instead of throwing punches, he charged forwards, head down and arms out ready to grab Buzzard. Again, Buzzard stepped aside, twisted so he was side on to the man, and used Cowmeadow's momentum — and his arm as a lever — to propel Cowmeadow into Molloy's wall.

The impact shook the whole room. A bottle fell from a shelf and smashed on the floor.

'Jesus,' somebody said.

A new ray of sunlight appeared between two planks in the wall.

'You broke my wall,' Molloy said.

It looked as if Cowmeadow's head

was stuck in the boards. For a few seconds he was motionless, bent over, arms swinging loosely beneath him.

Buzzard took several steps away from Cowmeadow. He'd thrown Cowmeadow into the wall harder than he'd meant to, but it was too late to stop now. He reached out and grabbed one of Molloy's chairs. If Cowmeadow still had any fight in him he was going to get a chair across the back of his head. There'd been a Japanese man back in Chicago who'd shown Buzzard how to fight this way. They'd worked together on the waterfront where being able to defend oneself had been just as important as it was out here on the frontier. It had been a long time since Buzzard had used these moves in anger and now that he had time to think about it — with Cowmeadow standing there, head down, one hand now pressed against the wall, holding himself upright — the Japanese man's main advice came flooding. *Run*, he'd said.

Any time you can avoid the fight, then avoid the fight.

Buzzard said, 'As I was saying, I don't know why you came in here so riled up. I don't even know you. But a bit of civility never goes amiss.'

Cowmeadow turned his head. There was a gouge on his forehead three inches long and blood ran down his face.

Molloy said, 'Oh Lord. Buzzard, you get now. Understand? Go.'

Buzzard looked at Molloy, then quickly back at Cowmeadow. The man's cheeks were burning with anger, but his eyes were glazed and unfocused. Cowmeadow reached up and wiped his face, looked at his bloodied hand.

Buzzard brought the chair into view. 'You want to talk in a civilized manner, I'll talk,' Buzzard said. 'You want to fight, I'll fight.' His Japanese mentor had also told him that any sign of weakness gave strength to an enemy. Sometimes you had to stand your ground.

Cowmeadow managed to pull himself to his full height again, but his legs were unsteady and he had to keep one hand against the wall.

'That fancy fighting . . .' he said, and stumbled out into the sunlight.

★   ★   ★

Buzzard's hand was shaking so much that he spilled the whiskey that Molloy poured him all over his sleeve and all over Molloy's counter.

'I thought you were a dead man,' Molloy said.

Buzzard's teeth clicked on the whiskey glass.

'He might be yet,' the man with the bowl of stew said.

'Give me another whiskey,' Buzzard said.

One of the old-timers said, 'Where d'you learn to fight like that, Buzzard? I never figured you for a fighting man.'

Buzzard downed the second whiskey. His arm stopped shaking.

'Who was that?' he said. 'I mean, *who* was he?'

'John Cowmeadow,' the stew man said. 'Runs a farm out West.'

'He was ... he seemed angry,' Buzzard said.

'John's always angry,' Molloy said. 'He used to blame his wife for his moods. These days it's his cattle or his cowboys; someone's always got him worked up or wanting to fight him over the blacks.'

Buzzard nodded.

'You might want to watch your step,' the stew man said. 'He won't take kindly to being taken the way you took him.'

'And he won't get caught twice,' the other old-timer said. 'I seen him kill a young cow once. With his bare hands.'

'I better have another drink,' Buzzard said.

'He tore the cow's throat out,' the old timer added.

5

There were 120 steps between Molloy's saloon and Kasey Christchurch's bunkhouse. Buzzard had counted them aloud one time when he was stumbling home. Did the fact that he'd been stumbling mean there were actually fewer steps than that? And had it been one hundred and twenty or two hundred and twenty? One hundred didn't seem that many.

He looked up at the moon, squinted. There were two of them. That was plainly wrong. He walked a little further, stepped down off the boards and on to the dirt and looked skyward again. Nope, still two moons. Maybe if he concentrated real hard he could make them coalesce . . . *Coalesce*. He smiled, and then giggled. That was a word you didn't hear in New Whitby very often. Certainly not one he'd use in company. Most people thought he talked a bit weird as it was. They didn't know much about him, that was the thing. They didn't know he could write. Or that he was educated. They didn't know he could fight.

Suddenly the two moons went out.

It was as if someone had dropped a curtain in front of them. A moment later he felt an arm around his neck. Another around his waist. He was lifted into the air, thrown to the ground. Someone kicked him in the belly. The wind exploded out of him. He struggled to breathe, sucking in the damp oats smell of a feedbag. Pain radiated from his stomach in great sick waves. He fought against vomiting, having to force himself to swallow whiskey-laden bile. He could hear them — two, maybe three men, whispering harshly. They tied his arms behind his back, and then he was in the air again, hearing the men breathing heavily as they ran with him. The smell of the horse feed filled his head, it whirled round within his skull and seemed to come out of his mouth and nose, and even ears and eyes.

Eyes.

He thought of Luther Curry hanging at Willow Canyon, his eyes gone.

He started to struggle, to twist and turn, he cried out, yelled as loud as he could.

Somebody clamped a hand over his mouth, forcing the burlap inside him. He gagged and thought he might choke. Someone punched him in the stomach again. The pain made him double up, but whoever had his legs held him tight. It felt as if his insides had split open. He tasted bile mixed with horse-feed now.

Then he heard the whinny of horses, smelled warm horseflesh, and they were heaving him over a saddle, slapping the animal's flanks, and were away, thundering over the hard ground, leaving the two moons somewhere far behind.

★ ★ ★

They left the sack over his head as they beat him. He didn't know whether not being able to see the punches was a good thing. After thirty seconds it didn't matter. His mouth and nose were bleeding, his stomach felt ruined, his ears were ringing. The pain had become a fog that he was sinking into. They were kicking him too, his arms and his legs — pulled up to protect his head — were receiving the worst of it.

When they stopped, the noise of his breathing — the sound of gritty air trying to find a way in and out of his lungs — was the loudest thing he'd ever heard. He could taste vomit and didn't know if he'd already been sick or was about to be. His heart seemed to be trying to smash its way through his ribs. He could feel tears on his face. Although he guessed it could have been blood.

'The others want to play all nicely, nicely,' someone said. He thought it was John Cowmeadow, but the whistling in his ears covered all the detail in the voice. 'Me, I just want to kill you bastards. Every damn one of you.'

Someone lifted him up. Maybe a couple of people. They pressed him against something hard. Maybe a tree. He thought of Luther Curry.

A knife slipped under the burlap bag they were using as a hood and pressed into his throat. He felt the skin split open.

'Who you sell Luther Curry's boots to?' someone asked. 'What did you find in 'em?' The voice came from several feet away from him. The person with the knife pressed it harder into his throat. The pain was more acute than any of the other pains coursing through his body, like a bright sun bearing down on a field of candles.

He thought of Luther Curry again, tortured to death and not giving anything away, despite the burning, and the taking of his eyes.

'I sold 'em to Rodney Purse,' he said. 'Down at the Mercantile. They were just boots, you son of a bitch. There was

69

nothing in 'em. They were just a pair of boots.'

There was a moment when nothing happened, then the hands holding him up left him, and he slipped to the floor. No one else said anything. He heard movement, heard men — several men — climbing on to horses, a few muttered 'gee-ups', and the sound of hoofs on hard ground.

Then he was alone, hood over his head, hand tied behind his back, his heart full of shame.

* * *

Rodney Purse rolled over on to his side, smiling.

'Maybe that'll do it,' he said.

In the bed beside him Lorna Purse murmured something.

'What's that?' Rodney said.

'I said, I think you might be right. It felt . . . '

'Good?'

'Oh yes,' she said. 'But it felt . . . special.'

Rodney smiled again. A warm breeze came through his open window, fluttered the curtains, and kissed the sweat away from his brow. Moonlight snuck in around the edges of the curtain and illuminated the room. Lorna snuggled into his back and wrapped an arm around him.

Someone started hammering on his door below.

'What's that?' Lorna said, rolling over on to her back. Rodney felt her body tense. His own heart started racing again, the way it had been just a few minutes ago, but this time for a different reason.

More hammering. Someone shouting for him to open up.

'Who is it?' Lorna said.

'I've no idea.'

He sat up.

'Don't go,' she said. 'I heard they've been pulling people out of their beds, shooting them in the street.'

The pounding on his door sounded heavy enough for whoever was doing it to break the latch any second.

'Not here,' he said. 'And, anyway, we ain't taken no sides. No one's got cause to drag us out.'

'Don't go!'

'Open up!' somebody called. 'Or we'll break the door down.'

'Who is it?' Lorna said again.

Rodney eased himself out of bed, took two steps and peered down from behind his curtains. There were two men down there that he could see. Both on horses; one of them was holding the reins of a third horse. The street was empty. Where was the sheriff when you wanted him?

'Who is it, Rod?'

'I don't know.'

The hammering started again. Now one of the riders looked up, saw Rodney, and then said something to the man hammering on his door.

'They've seen me,' Rodney said.

A big man walked into view.

'It's John Cowmeadow,' Rodney said. 'What does he want at this hour?'

72

Lorna said. 'That brute.'

'I better go down.'

'You tell him that we're closed, that whatever he wants he can wait till morning like the rest of them.'

Rodney slipped a coat over his shoulders.

'I'll be right back, honey.'

When Rodney opened the door John Cowmeadow pushed right past him and walked inside.

'It's the middle of the night, John,' Rodney said. 'I'm sure it's important but — '

'I heard you got a pair of boots for sale.'

'Boots? Well . . . yes. I've got several. But it's the middle — '

'I'm after the ones sold to you by Buzzard Jones.'

'Buzzard Jones?'

'I'm tired,' Cowmeadow said. 'It's been a long night.'

A shaft of moonlight came through the window, reflected off a selection of storage jars that Rodney had displayed there, and illuminated Cowmeadow's face. There was a dark mark on his forehead. It looked like dried blood.

'They're nice boots,' Rodney said. 'But — '

'Can I see 'em.'

Rodney sighed. 'I suppose so. Hold on.'

He went behind his counter, found an oil lantern and some matches. He replaced the glass over the burning wick and in the light he saw that he'd been right about the blood on Cowmeadow's face. There was a long deep gash on his forehead.

He went along to the far end of his counter and from a shelf at the back brought out the boots that Buzzard had sold him the day before yesterday.

Cowmeadow picked them up, shook them, turned them upside down.

'Was there anything in them?'

'In them? How do you mean?'

'I mean was there anything in them? You must still be asleep. You never kept a knife or a silver dollar in your boots?'

'No, sir.'

'Well, some people do.'

'If there was anything in these boots then Buzzard would know.'

'He says not.'

'How much are they?'

'Five dollars.'

'That's a lot of money for a pair of used boots.'

'Look at them, sir. Superior quality.'

'Five dollars?'

'Yes.'

'You know where they come from?'

'No.'

'They're a dead man's boots.'

A pause. 'They're good boots, sir.'

'They belonged to Luther Curry. He was a friend of mine. A good friend.'

'Oh no, they're not Luther's, sir. I was there when they brought Luther in. God bless his soul. Buzzard Jones brought these boots to me earlier that day, way before they found Luther Curry.'

★   ★   ★

Buzzard Jones figured he must have blacked out for a while. When he came round he could smell vomit and horse food. Could taste both of them, too, along with blood. His head ached. His legs ached. His body hurt. He arched his back and now the ache in his body turned into a searing pain. He slumped back on his hands, could feel the coarse rope binding them together. A cool breeze touched his chest, but inside the bag they'd put over his head his breath was hot.

He moved his head.

His neck hurt.

He sat forward again.

His spine hurt.

He stretched out his legs. At least they weren't tied.

He tried to get into a kneeling position but it hurt too much. Then he thought of Luther Curry hanging there, eyes gone, flesh burned, and he tried again. This time he made it. He leaned forward, and the movement made him feel sick. He leaned further forward, felt blood rushing into his head.

He shook his head.

But the sack wouldn't come off.

He tried to move his arms apart. There was scarcely any give in the rope. He sat upright again, felt something hard behind him — a tree, he figured — and he leaned on that.

He wondered where he was, and whether anyone would find him. How long that might take.

And who it might be.

★ ★ ★

'What did he want?' Lorna Purse said. 'I heard him yelling about some boots.'

Rodney Purse stood by the window looking down the street where Cowmeadow and his men had left dust hanging in the moonlight.

'He wanted to see the boots Buzzard Jones brought in.'

'The red pair?'

'Uh-huh.'

'In the middle of the night?'

77

'You know what he did? He took out a knife and he cut the heels open. I mean, he ruined them.'

'Why? What for?'

Rodney turned and looked at her.

'I don't know. There was nothing in them — I mean, I guess he was looking for something, but there was nothing. Just good leather.'

'I hope he paid for them.'

'He said . . . it was strange. He was angry, he said — '

'John Cowmeadow is always angry.'

'I know that. He said at first, when I asked him if he was going to pay, 'See Buzzard Jones. Get your money back off him.''

Rodney paused.

'Yes?' Lorna said. 'And?'

'Then he said, 'On second thoughts don't bother.' And he gave me the money. Five dollars.'

'Five dollars?'

'Five dollars.'

'Almost worth all the fuss.'

'I just . . . '

'What?'

'I like Buzzard,' Rodney said.

'What are you saying?'

'I think he's in trouble. When John went back outside he said to his cowboys, 'Let's go see Buzzard again. Get the full story *this* time.'

★ ★ ★

Buzzard Jones found that by pressing the back of his head hard up against the tree he could work the hood up an inch or two. The trouble was, each time he stopped pressing against the tree the hood fell back down. And it hurt too much to do it for more than a few seconds at a time. Hell, it hurt when he wasn't doing anything, let alone pressing his head against a gnarled tree trunk.

He tried again, got the same result, sighed, and let a wave of self-pity sweep over him. All he'd done was happen to ride upon a dying man. He'd done his best to help the poor fellow, and now look where he was.

'Life ain't fair, old buddy,' he said aloud, and the sound surprised him. He was still alive. That was his voice. He realized that he'd been sinking into a dark world where the only reality was pain and helplessness, and that the amount of pain was such that it made a man give up, that it was too much to cope with. But his voice, his own voice, the same voice he'd heard every day of his life through good times and bad, was still there, still strong, still alive. It brought him up from that darkness, like a bucket being hauled up from the cold dampness of a deep well. He thought of Luther Curry and the man's last request. Well, to hell with it, Buzzard thought. I *will* do what he asked of me. No one does all of this to Buzzard Jones and gets away with it.

It had been John Cowmeadow, for sure. The man had been humiliated by Buzzard in Molloy's and hadn't got the information he'd wanted. No one had spoken during the ride or the beating, so Buzzard guessed if the sheriff pushed him he wouldn't be able to say for sure that it had been the big man. But hell again, he knew, and anyway, there was no point in going to see Sheriff Toms. Jessica Day had been right, the guy was more interested in a free dinner and a nap than in seeing justice done.

Also, being hauled off the street and beaten was a damn sight better than being hauled out of bed and hanged and that was what was happening to a lot of people.

Buzzard had so far avoided the slavery issue. Not that he wasn't against it, but he had a living to make and it seemed foolish to alienate half of the people in the area.

But it was time to take a stand. Do what Luther Curry asked of him. Put some faith in the man's trust. Get back at the people who had beaten him, not through violence, but by helping the family Luther Curry had mentioned get up to Romego.

He laughed now, and though his

chest hurt, the sound had the same effect as his voice had a moment earlier. He felt alive and suddenly full of hope. Whatever Cowmeadow had been looking for wasn't in Luther's boots.

It had been in the man's last words.

Buzzard figured he'd need to get back to town, borrow some transport — maybe from Plymouth — and sneak out under cover of darkness. It would have to be tomorrow night now. He'd get on down to South Bottom Crossing and take this family up to Romego and the man called Powder.

See how John Cowmeadow liked that.

But first, he thought, flexing the knots around his hands and rotating his neck against the burlap hood. I have to get out of this lot.

* * *

It took an hour, or at least it felt like an hour. Buzzard Jones stood up, his back against the tree, and he leaned his skull hard against it and slowly worked his head down. He lost count of the number of times the hood started to reef up, then, the moment he let the pressure off, down it came again. So he worked his way around the tree, painfully searching for a roughness that would hook into the sacking. When at last he found it, it caught him by surprise. He started working his head downwards, feeling the sacking clear his mouth, his nostrils; he tasted the clear night air, started to see a change in the light, then stumbled, crashing to the floor. He cried out in pain, but found the hood was still hooked on to some rough bark on the tree.

He lay there, breathing heavily, shivering, realizing now how much he'd sweated.

Moonlight gave everything a silvery clean look. He was in a small hollow, where several trees grew in the lee of a rise. There were rocks and mesquite and a few yards away a jack rabbit looked at him, its ears and eyes alert. For a moment he thought he was in Willow Canyon, where he'd found Luther Curry, but no; this place was smaller.

He stood up again. The pain was lessening now, but he could feel his body stiffening. Bruises and tenderness was replacing punches and kicks. It must have been two hours, maybe more, since they'd beaten him. He tried to see over his shoulder at the knots around his wrist. It was no good. For a second he thought about rubbing the rope up and down the coarse bark of the tree. But that would take hours and he'd likely wear away his skin before the rope.

Back on the waterfront in Chicago the same guy who had shown him a few ways to fell bigger men had also shown him some other tricks, amongst them how to get out of a set of handcuffs. Well, the truth was, he'd never actually passed on the secret of springing the locks themselves, but he had shown Buzzard how to get the handcuffs from behind your back to in front of you, from where it was much easier to see what you were doing. It was pretty much common sense, when you thought about it, but it wasn't something Buzzard had ever had to think about until now.

He sat back down, and worked his tied hands as far down towards his ankles as he could. Getting them over his hips was the first problem. He wasn't a big man — totally the opposite — but it still wrenched his shoulders getting his hands down to his ankles. Once he'd got that far, he pulled his knees tight up against his chest, stretching his arms as far as he could, trying to get a heel hooked against a knot to give him leverage. He couldn't do it. His body, racked by new agony, just wouldn't become small enough. Sweat poured down his face. His clothes were soaked. Once, twice, ten times he had to stop, stretch out as best he could, and lie there letting the searing pains die down. He told himself he had no choice, but a renegade inner voice argued that he did — he could walk, couldn't he? He could walk with his hands tied behind his back and find somebody. What was wrong with that choice?

No. He wouldn't allow himself even to debate it. He could escape this. He would escape this.

He tried again, stretching his hands as far down towards his feet as he could, pulling his shoulders back, a grimace across his face. He tucked his knees so tightly into his chest that it was hard to breathe and . . . there! He hooked the edge of one heel into the gap between his wrists.

Thank God he never wore spurs, he thought. Had he needed another inch or two of clearance he would never have been able to make it.

He used the leverage now to pull his boots backwards and through his tied wrists.

The agony was worse than he could have imagined. It felt as if he was pulling his shoulders from their sockets, but a moment later his arms shot forward, his legs jack-knifed straight, and he lay there, tasting the dirt, panting with the effort, but with his tied hands in front of him.

He gave himself two minutes rest. No more. He hadn't gone through the agonies of the last hour to be caught if they came back looking for him.

The two minutes — well, maybe he'd taken three or four — done, he stood up and started walking up the side of the hollow, struggling to keep his balance. He picked at the knot as he went, twisting his fingers so that he could just get a little purchase on the rope. He looked at rocks and trees and scanned the ground for a sharp stone or anything that might help him.

Then he heard horses, approaching fast.

* * *

John Cowmeadow said, 'Son of a bitch! I knew we should have tied him to that tree.'

'We never figured on needing him again,' a man in a high-crowned black hat on a white-and-brown pinto said.

'Son of a bitch,' Cowmeadow said.

'He can't have got far,' another rider said. Buzzard lay as flat to the ground as he could. He'd hit the dust two seconds before the gang had ridden into sight. There were some low bushes, some rocks, and, behind him, the ground rising up preventing him from being silhouetted. He held his breath. 'Him with a hood on and his hands tied.'

'He ain't got a hood on no more,' Black Hat said. 'Look.' He was nodding at the tree.

'We been hours,' Cowmeadow said. 'He's gone. *Son of a bitch.* Someone must have found him.'

'He can't hide for ever.'

'We'll pick him up sooner or later.'

'That's too long. He knows something about tomorrow night. He must have spoken to Luther Curry before the man died. He stole Luther's boots way before they found the body.'

'What's today?' the third man asked.

'Friday,' Black Hat said.

'We need him,' Cowmeadow said. 'We got to find him by midday. There's no place to go round here. Especially if he's going to make a move. Raul, you head back to the ranch and rouse up the boys.'

'Ok, boss.'

'Me and Jacques are going back to town. We're going to find this sonofa-bitch.'

They turned and heeled their horses, leaving dust hanging in the air. Buzzard raised his head. They were already out of the hollow. He worked his way to the top of the rise, and saw the distant horsemen.

At least I know the way back to town, he thought. Beyond that he wasn't sure he knew much at all. Sometime during the beating the drunkenness had left him, but the punches and kicks had left him equally disorientated. All he was certain of was that he now had an absolute determination to act on Luther Curry's final words, to help this family get across the river and up to safety in Romego. What happened after that was beyond him, but he could do that much. He *would* do that much. He didn't know how, but he knew he couldn't do it alone. And that meant going back to town.

Right where Cowmeadow and his boys would be waiting.

6

Plymouth King was four feet down in the hole that would be Luther Curry's grave when he sensed movement above and behind him.

He turned and looked.

The world had a different perspective from such a low level. The rabbit view, he thought. The pile of dirt he'd excavated looked huge, rocks appeared bigger, grasses taller. His wagon, and the horse hitched to it, looked like an impossibly large creation.

But there was no one there.

Potter's Field was out at the north end of town. The trail to Romego curved north-west out of Whitby and the path to the cemetery ran off to the right where several trees grew together, giving shade to a growing number of graves. The ground was stony and hard, but at least you could dig a hole in it if you were prepared to put the work in. A lot of places round here, you dug down eighteen inches and it was rock. Plymouth liked to dig the graves in the early dawn before anyone was around. His jacket was hanging on one of the low tree branches and sweat was already working its way through his undershirt. It wasn't the image he liked to portray, yet he still liked to do the digging. He made the coffins, and he dressed the dead, if necessary. It seemed right that he should dig their graves, too. He'd planted some grass and some flowers up at the Field, too. Neither was taking very well, but, given some rain, he still held hope that the place would soon be less desolate. It seemed the least he could do. Others were putting up buildings in town, laying plankwalks, digging wells. Some were bringing things in to town — Luther, here, rest his soul had driven in with two pianos not so long ago, and had brought in an entire printing-press a time before that. They had a dentist now, albeit he was still working out of a tent, and every time somebody finished a boarding-house or a hotel then it seemed to be filled overnight. Yes, the town was suddenly growing fast, and it seemed only fair that he should do his bit to make it a little bit more civilized, a little bit more permanent, a little prettier even.

'Plymouth.'

He jumped, then turned again.

Buzzard Jones stepped out from behind one of the trees. From this level he had a good view of Buzzard's boots. The man looked about eighteen feet tall.

'Thank . . . the Lord,' Buzzard said. 'I guessed that you might be burying Luther today and that you'd be here.'

He dropped down into the grave alongside Plymouth, and let out a painful gasp.

'My God,' Plymouth said. 'What happened to you?'

Buzzard's clothes were torn and dirty — it looked like a mixture of blood, sweat, and dust. His face was equally filthy, but it was also red with cuts and swellings. Some of the lumps were already turning blue. His eyes seemed deeper in his face than normal, as if he'd seen something that was haunting him. And his hands were tied in front of him.

'John Cowmeadow,' Buzzard said, casting a look over his shoulder, seemingly forgetting he was hidden from view. He hunched down as if hiding from somebody.

'John Cowmeadow? He wouldn't — '

'Can you cut through the rope, Plym?'

Buzzard held his hands out. His wrists were bleeding.

'You need to see the doctor — '

'No!'

'Buzzard . . . '

'I can't go into town. They're waiting for me.'

'What's going on?'

'If I put my hands on the ground can you cut through the rope?'

Buzzard crouched down and held his hands out in front of him, pulling them apart as far as the rope would allow, which wasn't much.

'Don't hurt me,' Buzzard said, and began to laugh.

Plymouth drove his spade through the rope. It took three goes before he'd severed the knot. As Buzzard stood up, still looking around him as if every breath of wind that whispered over the top of the grave was someone coming for him, the cut ropes fell from his wrists.

'What happened?' Plymouth said.

★ ★ ★

Mary Colton thought there was something about Buzzard Jones. She couldn't quite put her finger on it, but it was something good. Maybe it was the pleasant surprise of finding a man — a handsome man, no less — who could actually read and write, who was *learned*, in this place. But even if it was that, there was something more. There was a sensitivity to him. Sure, he needed to come out and position himself firmly in the camp of the abolitionists. No right-thinking man, no *learned* man, could surely have pro-slavery leanings? But when he spoke, there was a depth to him. A depth that few seemed to be aware of. And the fact that he didn't seem to care what the majority of people thought of him only added to the mystery.

Mary was up early. She'd closed the school today, on account of Luther Curry's funeral, but still wanted to spend a couple of hours sweeping the dust out of the classroom, repainting the door where the wind and grit had stripped much of the colour, and to draw some animals on the blackboard ready for Monday. Her drawing skills were not good and she knew it was going to take several attempts at each one. It was something she'd rather do alone, rather than in front of a dozen laughing children.

Someone was calling her name.

She looked round. Kasey Christchurch was walking towards her, smiling. But there was something behind that smile, something hard.

'Kasey,' she said. 'Good morning.'

'You're up early,' Kasey said.

'Schoolhouse chores.'

'I wanted to ask . . . ' Kasey paused, and already Mary knew that this was going to be about Buzzard. Did Kasey have feelings for him? Was there something between them? Had she, Mary, done something wrong yesterday by marching him down the street with her arm in his?

'Yes?'

'Sam . . . *Buzzard* never came home last night. I was wondering . . . '

Mary thought how attractive Kasey was. Her red hair lent a stroke of brightness in a dull landscape, her smile was pretty, her clothes clean and her figure fine.

'No,' she said, feeling a twinge of jealousy — for what, she wasn't sure.

'He wasn't . . . I mean . . . '

'I'm worried,' Kasey said. 'Bill Carson, one of my boarders, said he'd heard Buzzard was in a fight yesterday. With John Cowmeadow.'

Mary thought of Cowmeadow storming from their meeting with the intention of finding out what Buzzard had done with Luther Curry's boots. She hadn't seen Cowmeadow since. A shiver ran down her spine.

'John Cowmeadow?' she said, unable to think of any other words as her mind conjured up an image of Cowmeadow beating Buzzard to a pulp. John was a good man politically. He was absolutely behind what they were doing. Sometimes he even allowed his ranch to be used as a staging post for hiding runaway slaves. But he had a vicious temper and was a bully.

'Apparently Buzzard embarrassed him,' Kasey said.

'Buzzard did?' The shiver turned to warmth across her shoulders. But it was warmth tempered with confusion.

'Apparently so. Supposedly, he won the fight. Knocked John Cowmeadow out is what Bill heard. But then he didn't come home. I was hoping he was . . . with you.'

If Kasey Christchurch was *hoping* that Buzzard was with me then maybe there isn't anything between them, Mary thought. Not that there's anything between us. But it was still good to understand the landscape.

'No,' she said.

'Because if not . . . ' Kasey reached out and put her hand on Mary's elbow, pulled her into the early morning shadows alongside Rodney Purse's store. 'I fear that John Cowmeadow, bully that he is, may have done something. You know, to get his own back.'

'I'm not sure that John — '

'You know him?'

Mary thought about it. Did she *really* know him?

'No,' she said.

'You see,' Kasey said, 'there's something in the air this morning.'

'What do you mean?'

'I mean I saw John Cowmeadow not five minutes ago, riding through town. Then back again. And over there, down where they're starting the hotel, there's another man, just sat watching the trail.'

Mary looked. It took her a few seconds but then her eyes found the cowboy on horseback waiting in the alleyway beside the partly erected building.

'They're looking for someone,' Kasey said. 'And I think it's probably Buzzard.'

★   ★   ★

'So I need to borrow your wagon and horse,' Buzzard said.

'To go and take this family to Romego?' Plymouth said. Buzzard had told him everything that had happened in Willow Canyon, and most that had happened since. They were still crouched down in Luther Curry's grave.

100

'Uh-huh.'

'You won't make it.'

'I will.'

'Look at you. You need patching up. You need to sleep.'

'Plym, they tortured that man to death. They would have done the same to me.'

'And now they're looking for you. You think the one place they *won't* be watching is the Missouri trail?'

'I've got no choice. I have to do it.'

'I'm burying Luther Curry at midday,' Plymouth said. 'I need the wagon then.'

'And afterwards?'

'You won't make it.'

'Plym . . . '

Plymouth reached up and took his spectacles off, peered at them, then used the corner of his shirt to wipe them clean. He looked up at Buzzard with naked eyes.

'Unless . . . '

'Unless what?'

'You sure it's John Cowmeadow? I

mean, who Luther was talking about?'

'One hundred per cent. I mean, you said it — look at me.'

Plymouth nodded. He slipped his glasses back on, adjusting the legs so they were comfortable behind his ears.

'What is it, Plym?' Buzzard said.

'I'll help you,' Plymouth said. 'No one'll suspect me. I'll go and get the family.'

'Don't be crazy. It's too dangerous — '

'No. Not if you act as a decoy.'

Buzzard frowned, then nodded.

'It could work. But I still don't like it. I didn't come here to involve you.'

'I'm like you, Buzz,' Plymouth said. 'I have to keep all sides happy in order to make a living. But sooner or later one has to nail one's colours to the mast.'

'Nail one's colours to the mast,' Buzzard repeated, as if trying the phrase out for size.

'It's a nautical phrase,' Plymouth said.

Buzzard nodded again. 'We need a plan.'

Plymouth said, 'It's a pretty long ride to South Bottom Crossing. As soon as the funeral is done I'll go home and change and set off.'

'What I can do,' Buzzard said, 'is wait until everyone's up here paying their last respects. Then I'll sneak into the livery and get my horse.'

'Ride past the funeral party?' Plymouth said.

'I'll be up on the rise. Heading towards the river, but north.'

'I'll make sure they see you,' Plymouth said.

'Soon as they do I'll ride like the wind.'

'But where? You can't run for ever.'

'I'll head for Herb's. It's a few hours — '

'It's more than a few.'

'Yeah. But given a good start I can make it. Ol' Herb's still got the guns the army issued us. Anyone wanting to fight . . . well, it'll be just like old times.'

'You take Cowmeadow and his men three, four hours to the west and I can get down to the river unseen.'

Buzzard smiled. 'I think we've got a plan.' Then his smile straightened. 'But really, I never meant to involve you, Plym.'

'My bit is easy. Just don't let them catch you.'

'I won't.'

'Come on, you can't hide here. I'm putting Luther in this hole in a few hours. Climb into the back of my wagon. There's a tarp there. You can clean yourself up and hide out at my place until it's time to go.'

Buzzard looked at Plymouth.

'What?' Plymouth said.

'Nothing. Just . . . thanks, buddy.'

7

At the back of the schoolhouse was a small office. Mary Colton had a desk in the office on which she wrote letters to her friends and family. She had a cupboard in which she kept paper and ink, chalk and dusters, some bandages and needles and threads. There were cups and saucers that she'd never used and a pair of red shoes with high heels that Luther Curry had brought back for her from one of his trips. She'd never worn them in public. Leaning against the side of the cupboard was a broom and, on the floor, a dustpan and brush. Above her desk a window looked out across the street. From the window she could see the church, and she could see Molloy's saloon and the sheriff's office. The door from her office gave a slightly different view. And it was from this door, when she was crouched down emptying the dust from the dustpan, that she saw Plymouth King pull up at the back of his property, look around, then walk to the rear of his cart and pull a tarp free from off the wagon. Then she saw Buzzard Jones rise slowly — looking as if he was in pain — from the flatbed of the wagon and quickly limp through Plymouth's back door.

It happened so quickly that she almost thought that it might be imagination brought on from the conversation that she'd had with Kasey Christchurch.

But she wasn't a girl who was prone to imaginings.

She came back in, closed the door, and leant against it. What was going on? John Cowmeadow and Buzzard Jones had reputedly fought — no doubt over the boots that John was making a big fuss about, crazy as it seemed. And, if Kasey was to be believed, Buzzard had somehow got the best of that fight, crazy as that seemed too. But now he was in hiding — and Plymouth King was helping him. All this two days after Luther was murdered. There had to be a connection. She thought back to her conversation with Buzzard — he'd been open and, as far as she could tell, honest. He showed her everything that he'd picked up. More important, he'd been clear about where his allegiance lay — to himself. She thought herself a good judge of character and really didn't believe that Buzzard Jones had anything to do with Luther's death. So why was John Cowmeadow so anxious to get to him? Surely it was more than just pride over a fight.

An anger came over her. She was part of this organization. She risked her life to help John and Father Wiseman and Lloyd and . . . Luther. Why did she feel as if she'd been excluded from something important here?

It had to be about this weekend. *This evening*. That was the one thing of which she was sure. Luther hadn't been killed by chance. He'd been planning something big — had them all lined up to help him once he was sure that it was going to go ahead. He hadn't told them anything yet, said it was too big, too important, that this crossing would be the one that broke open the story, the *real* story.

And so he had been killed.

But who knew about it, aside from the four of them? Unless the killers came from Missouri? There was always that possibility. But she could do nothing about that. What she could influence was what happened this side of the river. It seemed clear that the answer, or at least information that might lead to the answer, lay with Buzzard and John Cowmeadow.

She stared out of the window at the church. Plymouth would be at Luther's service, as would John, and the rest of them. She would be, too. But maybe, if she could time it right, she could find a moment between the service and the burial to slip over to Plymouth's house.

And ask Buzzard Jones some questions.

★ ★ ★

The turnout was greater than Plymouth had expected. Maybe the nature of Luther Curry's death had moved a few more people to pay their respects than usual. Or maybe Luther simply had dealings with a lot more people than Plymouth had realized. The man had forever been organizing wagon trains from the East, often travelling with them. He'd brought in a fair amount of lumber and tools for Plymouth himself over the last few years. Even the wagon that Plymouth now owned came from Luther.

John Cowmeadow, Lloyd Avery, Jackson Arnold from the livery, and Gunther Krug, who, like Luther, made his fortune by bringing goods from wherever to this dusty child of a town, carried the coffin into the small church. Father Wiseman presided over the service. It wasn't a long service, but it was very moving. Wiseman painted a picture of a Luther Curry whom few in the congregation had been aware of. He had a wife, Bella, back home in Virginia to whom he returned as often as he could. He'd promised Bella that he would trade out in the west for three years, make his fortune, and then come home to raise a family. His three-year deadline had been just a few months away. His fortune, so far as Wiseman knew, had already been made. He could have gone home for good earlier, but this last year Luther Curry had found an additional mission in his life — he'd become a keen supporter of the abolitionists. Wiseman had had to raise his hands and call for quiet at this point. 'I know we're on the crossroads of opinion right here in Kansas,' he said. 'But please, whatever your views, let us consider the sacrifice that Luther Curry made for his beliefs. He will never go home to Bella. They will never raise a family together. But, it's no exaggeration to say that others will because of what Luther did.'

Afterwards, the four pallbearers loaded the coffin back on to Plymouth's wagon.

'Nice service,' Lloyd Avery said.

John Cowmeadow said, 'Shouldn't have to be burying Luther at all. Somebody's going to pay, that's for sure.'

*   *   *

Buzzard knew he should never have lain down. The pains and the aches coursing through his body were bearable whilst he kept moving, whilst his mind was on other things. But the moment he stopped and lay down to rest — even for just half an hour — it was almost impossible to start again.

Plymouth had helped him wash and had given him clean pants — albeit they were slightly too big — and a fresh shirt, then Plymouth had gone to prepare Luther's coffin, and get ready for the service.

Buzzard lay on Plymouth's bed and listened to the undertaker talking to some men outside — whoever it was that he had organized to help him carry the coffin. A little while later his friend geed-up the horses, the church bell — which always sounded very small to Buzzard — tolled several times, and then there was quiet.

He gave it ten minutes, then tried to rise.

His belly ached. His limbs hurt as much now as when the punches and kicks had been going in. His neck and shoulders felt as if someone had driven nails into them.

But what were a few bruises compared to having your eyes scooped out?

He forced himself to stand, and once he'd got his balance and the sick feeling had passed he forced himself to put on his boots and jacket.

Then he carefully walked downstairs.

Plymouth had said to him, 'Buzz, I know you're not one for guns, but there's a Colt '51 on the table. Take it. You don't even have to use it, but just having it might be useful.'

Buzzard Jones wrapped the gunbelt around his waist, adjusted it best he could, and then, limping now, with the gun rising up and slapping the outside of his thigh with every step, he eased himself out of Plymouth's door, crossed the street, and hurried down to the livery.

★ ★ ★

Plymouth King helped the pall-bearers slide Luther's coffin on to the back of his wagon. Then he walked around to the front, climbed in, gave the reins a little shake, and set off slowly through the town of New Whitby towards his graveyard with a small group of people walking behind him. Plymouth kept his eyes straight ahead as he passed the livery, but still he imagined that he could see Buzzard in there, sitting astride his horse, waiting. Buzzard would head out of town in the opposite direction, work his way around to the high ground, and then . . .

Then he would have to ride as if the Devil himself was on his tail.

And maybe that wasn't so far from the truth.

* * *

Buzzard left it long enough for the burial party to make it halfway up the hill then, heart pounding and muscles still aching he climbed on to the horse. The plan, which had seemed so workable when he and Plymouth had been crouched down in Luther's grave now felt too simplistic. He had to ride long enough and hard enough to give Plymouth time to get home, get changed, and roll out of town at an easy, unobtrusive pace. But what then? He'd been party to the successes of enough posses to know that a group of riders almost always caught a lone man.

That was the trouble when you had to make plans under pressure, when you were reacting to circumstances rather than creating them.

He thought back to his dockyard days, and the friend who had taught him to fight and had advised him to run. The Japanese man had also told him to do the unexpected. If you've got no other options, then surprise is your last friend, the man had said. If nothing else, seeing him up there on the ridge above Plymouth's graveyard was going to be a hell of a surprise.

Buzzard checked that the bag containing several chunks of bread and some beef jerky was tied securely on to the back of his saddle. The way he figured it, he might have to lie low somewhere for a while and he didn't want to starve.

But he hoped it wasn't going to come to that. Herb's wasn't that far away. And so long as he made it there then he'd be fine. He and Herb had taken on the Mexicans. A pro-slavery farmer whom he'd already beaten in one fight wasn't going to be a problem.

He clicked his heels against his horse's flanks and walked her out into the sun.

Mary Colton was standing there, waiting for him.

Aiming a tiny handgun right at him.

8

'My father gave me it,' she said. 'A going-away present when he realized I absolutely meant it when I told him I was coming West to do some good. It's a Derringer. It might look small, but I assure you, I'm not afraid to use it.'

'I thought we were getting on so well,' he said. He tried to sound calm, but there was tension in his shoulders. He didn't have time for this.

She smiled.

'Don't take this the wrong way. I just want some answers, that's all. You probably don't know it, but there's a lot at stake.'

'I do know,' he said.

'What's going on?' she said. 'Do you know that?'

'I need to leave,' he said. He looked up the street. The burial party was up in Plymouth King's little graveyard. 'Now.'

116

'Not before you tell me what's going.' She raised the gun another inch and held it out before her as if to emphasize the point. 'What happened to you? Your face . . .'

He stared at her, trying to work out how much, if at all, he could trust her.

'People are going to see you, if you're not careful,' he said. 'See the school-marm holding a gun on Buzzard Jones.'

She brought her hands closer to her chest, so the gun was less visible.

'When I couldn't find you at Plymouth's house,' she said, 'I thought you might be leaving town.'

'You knew I was at Plymouth's?'

'Why is John Cowmeadow so desperate to get to you?'

'I beat him in a fight.'

'It's more than that. It's about Luther Curry, isn't it?' Maybe something flashed across his face because she quickly followed this with, 'You know where the crossing is, don't you? Luther told you.'

'I don't know what you're talking about.'

'That's it,' she said. 'That explains the boots.'

'The boots?'

'He was still alive when you took the boots off him. They brought him in but you'd already sold the boots on.'

There were red patches on her cheeks. Her grey eyes were wide with anger. He knew he should have just ridden away. He doubted she'd shoot him. But afterwards, all being well, he would be back here. And he still remembered the way it had felt to have her arm in his, have the prettiest girl in town walking with him. And she looked particularly beautiful now, dressed in black for the funeral service.

'I'm not a thief,' he said.

She stared at him.

'They tortured him,' he said. 'Whoever they are. Southerners, I guess. By the time I got there he was as good as dead.'

'You stole his boots.'

'The money is put aside for Bella. You know that. I already explained.'

'He was dying and you stole his boots. Did you steal his hat and jacket, too.'

Now he was angry. 'There was too much blood on them.'

'And to think . . . '

'To think what?' he said.

She looked at him. 'Nothing.'

'What were you going to say?'

'Nothing, Buzzard Jones.'

He stared back at her. She'd lowered the gun now, but her face was still red with anger at him.

'Yes, Luther Curry told me something,' he said.

She closed her eyes briefly, then sighed, and opened her eyes again.

'You know, don't you?'

Buzzard nodded.

'But he told me not to trust anyone.'

'Yet *he* trusted a thief.'

'I guess he was a better judge of character than you.'

'What's that meant to mean?'

'It means you ought to let me explain.'

'Forget it. This is more important than us.'

'Us?'

'You know what I mean.'

'I need to go,' he said. 'You know as much as I do now.'

She raised the gun. 'Like hell I do.'

He couldn't help but smile. The gun was so small. It looked like a toy.

'What?' she said.

He shook his head.

'John Cowmeadow,' she said.

'What about him?'

'Why is he after you?'

'I figure he believes I know something.'

'He's right.'

'Yep. And so he wants to stop me doing something with this knowledge.'

'Maybe,' she said. 'John's a good man. Maybe he just wants to know what Luther told you. The same as we all do.'

'All?'

'The same as I do.'

'I've already told you too much. You

120

could be the one.'

'The one?'

'The one I shouldn't trust.'

She shook her head. 'No, it's not me.' The fire in her cheeks had faded slightly. He'd liked the way she'd said the one as if she'd misunderstood what he'd been getting at.

'I've got to go, Mary,' he said. 'Before it's too late.'

'You won't do it on your own,' she said. 'They'll need transport.'

He smiled, pressed his heels into his horse's flanks and rode away from her, an itch in the small of his back where her bullet would go if she decided to shoot him.

* * *

Not quite as many people came up the hill as had gone to the church. The sun was getting high and there was a hot and dusty wind blowing from the west. Father Wiseman said a few more words. Everybody bowed their heads to pray.

Plymouth glanced up.

John Cowmeadow was looking around, too. His face was drawn. There was a nasty bruise on his forehead.

After the prayer was finished Father Wiseman threw a handful of dirt on to Luther Curry's coffin. Several other people did the same. The burial was almost done.

Where was Buzzard?

Plymouth leaned forward and dropped a handful of dry dirt into the grave. He heard it rattle on top of the wooden coffin lid. Then he stepped back and surreptitiously glanced up at the ridge again.

Still no sign of him.

Wiseman was saying how it was a terrible waste, off the record now, no longer the priest, now the friend telling how some son-of-a-bitch ought to hang for doing what they did to such a good man. It was strange hearing the priest talk this way. Almost as if it were someone else.

And then there he was, up on the rise

facing north, close enough for anyone to see that it was clearly Buzzard Jones, far enough way for no one to be able to get to him, not without first working their way up to the ridge.

Plymouth stared at Buzzard, then quickly ran his eyes around the small crowd. No one else had noticed.

Come on, he thought. *Look up.*

John Cowmeadow was looking down at the coffin, Lloyd Avery was talking to Father Wiseman. Gunther Krug had already turned away and was walking towards the little gate that Plymouth had put up at the entrance to Potters Field. The fence around the graveyard wasn't yet complete, but he thought the gate added some gravitas to the setting. Jackson Arnold was talking to Sheldon Molloy.

All night and day someone — almost certainly Cowmeadow, but maybe some of the others, too — had been searching for Buzzard and now that he'd shown himself none of them had even noticed.

Plymouth King coughed into his

hand, then said aloud, 'Buzzard Jones. Son-of-a-bitch, you're alive.'

★ ★ ★

Buzzard Jones had never considered himself a hero. Even when he'd followed his old friend Herb Jordan down to fight in the Mexican War he'd not really felt particularly heroic. The truth was he'd never really seen a Mexican. Not close up and not alive. There'd been a battle — a lot of rifle shooting from high up, their entire section being in the rocks. It had been an ambush, in which they'd slaughtered a Mexican wagon train. But whereas Herb had gone on to become a real hero, even mentioned back in Washington — well, according to Herb himself — Buzzard had simply found himself at the tail-end of the army at the tail-end of the war. Strangely, whilst in the army, he'd never ever felt as though he was in danger. Eventually he'd drifted away altogether and rambled for several years. Going back to Chicago, coming West again, and ultimately settling down here, in New Whitby, not because Herb had a place close by, but enjoying the coincidence. There'd been a few fights over the years, too. Quite a few victories in Chicago's docklands, probably an equal amount of defeats, too. And there was the beating of that brute John Cowmeadow in Molloy's saloon just a day ago. But fist-fights were a different prospect from setting yourself up as bait in a game where death — probably your own — was the penalty for losing. His body still ached. He felt weary and his concentration was wavering. He no longer believed in this plan. He wasn't even sure he should even have got himself involved. How had he got involved? The events were too confusing to work out. And then there was Mary Colton. Mary with the grey eyes and who smelled so clean and womanly. Mary with the smile that would surely turn any man into a fool. He could have told her everything.

Explained it all. Instead she believed him to be a thief. Hell, he *was* a thief. But not in the way she saw him. And maybe trying to prove otherwise to Mary was the reason — or one of the reasons — why he was doing this.

He stared down at the funeral party. No-one was looking his way. Most of them were looking into Luther Curry's grave.

Buzzard's belly gurgled. He felt sick. He spat on the ground.

Come on. Let's get this thing started.

Then he saw Plymouth King look up at him.

A moment passed and then they all looked at him.

He saw John Cowmeadow's mouth open, some words were said. The wind was in the wrong direction for Buzzard to pick them up.

Then John Cowmeadow pulled his jacket aside, grabbed a gun from his waist band and fired at Buzzard.

Buzzard had no idea where the bullet went. He wasn't hit and he didn't hear anything. But suddenly everything seemed too real. They wanted him dead. Properly dead. Just because he'd happened upon a pair of boots.

Cowmeadow fired again.

This time Buzzard heard the whistle of a bullet.

He jabbed his heels into his horse, leant as low over her neck as he could, and started galloping to the north.

Another gunshot sounded.

He risked a look over his shoulder and saw Cowmeadow pointing his gun directly into the air.

Damn. Damn. Damn.

Buzzard had figured that by the time John Cowmeadow had made it back into town and rounded up his boys, he — Buzzard — would have several miles lead. At worst, he could get across the scrublands and into the hills and lose his pursuers. At best he'd make it all the way to Herb Jordan's ranch — Herb Jordan whom he'd been on his way back from visiting when all of this kicked off. Herb Jordan who still insisted he single-handedly beat the Mexicans. It would be interesting to see what John Cowmeadow made of Herb. The chances were they'd already met — but never when one of them was trying to kill the other's friend.

All of which was suddenly irrelevant.

John Cowmeadow's gunshots had served as a signal. Already there were several riders kicking up dust on the outskirts of town as they raced after Buzzard.

9

Every stride that his horse made felt like a hammer blow somewhere within his battered body. Yet he urged her on. He was kicking up a dust storm behind him that somehow still filled his own mouth with grit. Several times he looked round but his pursuers were out of sight now. At least he had a little lead on them.

But the question came with every jarring stride: *was it enough?*

The plan had faltered at its first stage. Somehow he had to buy Plymouth enough time to get down from the graveyard, into town, to get changed, and to take what looked like a leisurely ride out of town.

He urged his horse on. As he rose in the saddle and looked backwards again he felt the strange weight of the gun on his hip. Could he really outrun several riders? Maybe a better bet would be to find a place he could hole up, try and hold them off for a few hours. At least that way Plymouth would get the time he needed.

But that way meant no escape, and Buzzard didn't know whether he had the courage to sacrifice himself.

He rode on, the horse sliding on stones.

A broken leg now and none of it would matter anyway.

He topped a ridge, looked backwards and saw Cowmeadow's riders — three of them — about a mile and a half, maybe two, behind him.

It was further than he thought.

Maybe he was making better time than they.

Maybe they were pacing themselves.

Maybe he could make it.

Maybe.

He turned his horse, heading deeper into Kansas territory, rather than towards the river. He'd circle to the north-west. All the time working his way closer to Herb Jordan's ranch.

But he could already feel the horse slowing. Her breathing was still fast and loud but her legs couldn't keep up the pace. Her flanks were wet with sweat. His own sweat soaked through his shirt and pants, dripping down from beneath his hat. His own heart pounded in his chest.

He raced along a dry gully, thankful that it was summertime. In winter the gully would have been four feet deep in water. In a wet winter anyway.

Several hundred yards along the dry riverbed he turned the horse up the grassy slope, into a rare copse of trees, the sudden shade feeling cool on his burning skin. Slowing now, he worked her through the woodland, out the other side. Here the grassland undulated across to some low hills several miles away.

He stopped just for a moment, looked around. They probably weren't yet into the gully, let alone the woods.

He thought about working his way

quietly forward, turning back on them, trying to trick them.

But that was crazy. Stick to the original plan, Buzzard, he told himself.

He had to cross the open land, get through the hills, and press on to Herb's.

'Let's go,' he said, feeling the itch in the small of his back that he'd first imagined when he'd ridden away from Mary Colton, a gun in her hand.

He raced out into the open.

★ ★ ★

Mary Colton slipped the Derringer back into her purse and watched Buzzard ride out of town. The gun hadn't even been loaded. The truth was it was such a convoluted thing to set up that she'd only ever done it twice — both times shortly after her father had first given it to her. She couldn't ever imagine actually shooting anyone, but especially not Buzzard. Somehow she couldn't shake the conviction that he was a good man, that he was telling the truth whilst, at the same time, not telling her the most important part of it — where the crossing was, and who Luther Curry had arranged to bring over. She understood Buzzard's reason, too. Luther had told him not to trust anyone, and so he was going to try and do it on his own. But look at him now, he looked so small against the huge sky, a speck of nothing against the rocks and the plains. At least they — she and Father Wiseman and Lloyd and John — had each other, had an organization. What could Buzzard Jones do on his own?

She watched him a while longer, the dust hanging in the air, behind him. He was riding fast, too fast to keep it up for very long. She didn't know a great deal about horses, but she understood that they were living creatures and susceptible to the same fatigue as any other beast.

He turned now, just as she glanced away.

Where was he going? She lost sight of

him for a moment behind the hotel that was being erected at the edge of town. She walked across the street, down the side of the hotel, the smell of newly sawn timbers and someone brewing coffee rising up from the workings.

There he was. He was working his way up to the high ground beyond the grave-yard.

Surely they'd see him. If John Cowmeadow was after Buzzard why on earth was he showing himself that way? John was right up there with the burial party. She should have been there, too. She suspected they'd ask questions later. But somehow, seeing Buzzard had been more important. Luther would have understood.

It looked as though the interment was almost done. Even from this distance she could see the mourners throwing dirt down into the grave.

And then there was Buzzard, high above them, as clear as could be.

A moment later John Cowmeadow started shooting at him.

Plymouth King, out of his best suit now, but still looking smart, climbed back up on to the wagon seat, lifted the reins, and was just about to say 'git on gone' to his horse when Mary Colton jumped up and sat on the seat alongside him.

'Mary,' he said.

She still had on the black jacket she'd worn to the church service. Her cheeks looked slightly flushed. She looked as if she'd either been running or was excited about something.

'School's closed,' she said. 'I thought it would be a nice day for a ride.'

'I . . . uh . . . '

'I don't care where,' she said, and smiled. Plymouth suddenly felt very old. It was a sad feeling, a moment when his youth — all those years ago — flashed through his mind. There'd been pretty girls, sure, but none as pretty as Mary Colton. That flush on her cheeks; the way her hair was neat, but a little windswept and wild at the same time. Those eyes. The melancholy settled on his shoulders, but then she smiled again and asked him where he was headed, and he felt warm and good.

'I need lumber,' he said. 'For coffins.'

'Can't you get one of the — '

'Luther used to bring it in for me,' he said. 'God rest his soul.'

She crossed herself.

'I saw you at the church,' he said.

'I wanted to pay my respects.'

'Were you close?' he asked.

'Plymouth?'

The way she said it, her grey eyes looking earnestly at him, he knew there was trouble coming.

'What is it, Mary?'

'Buzzard told me everything,' she said.

'Buzzard told you — '

'Everything.'

'He did, did he?'

'Uh-huh.'

Plymouth dropped the reins into his lap.

'What exactly did he tell you?'

'He told me that Luther Curry was still alive when Buzzard found him. That he'd told Buzzard where the crossing was and that John Cowmeadow was a traitor. I mean, a traitor to us — you know, the abolitionists.'

'He told you that?'

'And he said that he was going to act as a . . . decoy, was the word Buzzard used, to enable you to slip out of town and go and help these poor souls across the river and to freedom.'

'Buzzard said that?'

'I saw John Cowmeadow shooting at him.'

'Yes, that was something of a surprise.'

'You hadn't planned for that?'

'No. I mean . . . Buzzard really told you everything?'

'He trusts me,' she said. 'I wanted to help. To go with him, but he said it was far too dangerous. He said if I wanted to do something to help — you know, that's what I do. I've done this before, he said to come and find you. To ride with you.'

Plymouth nodded. He looked into those deep eyes. It was inconceivable she'd be lying. She knew too much.

'We'd better get a move on. It's a long way to South Bottom. You got a coat? It'll be cold by midnight.'

'I'm OK. I've got this jacket.'

'There's an old saddle blanket in the back. Some water and some corn bread, too.'

She smiled. 'You're a good man, Plymouth.'

'I'm a damn fool, that's what I am.'

Now she laughed.

'Plymouth, tell me about Buzzard,' she said.

Plymouth King stared at her for a moment, then he looked back to his horse. He snapped the reins. 'Git on gone,' he said, and together they pulled out.

★ ★ ★

Buzzard Jones heeled his horse on, urging her ever further, ever faster, although the latter was just wishful thinking now. She'd settled into a rhythm, a steady lope. He hoped it was a faster rhythm than those behind him. Dust caked his face and dried his eyes. Every time he blinked he could feel the grit scratching his eyes. The inside of his mouth felt full of dirt and he found it hard to even produce enough saliva to spit the dirt out. Yet, his body, like that of his horse, was bathed in sweat. The mid-afternoon sun bore down with no respite. At one point he'd stopped, taken a long drink from his water-skin, filled his hat with water, and given it to his horse, who lapped it up thirstily. When he'd put his hat back on the remaining water ran down his neck and cooled him for a few seconds. But after he started riding again he found it was impossible to get his horse up to the same speed again.

How long had he been riding for?

He looked up at the sun. Two hours?

Maybe two and a half. It wasn't long enough and they hadn't got far enough. Herb's ranch, normally a day's gentle ride, was still a few hours away even at this speed. And though his pursuers hadn't yet gained on him, whenever he'd crested a rise and looked backwards there'd they'd been, small figures in the distance, still coming on relentlessly. In fact, there seemed to be more of them now. A growing posse. Maybe John Cowmeadow himself had caught up with them. Maybe that was why he'd gapped them — they were riding slowly, waiting for the big man to catch up.

His horse stumbled.

It caught itself, regained balance, and carried on, but the sign was clear. Exhaustion was approaching fast.

He started to think that she was limping. For a while he convinced himself that he'd ridden her too hard, ruined her. But then she seemed to find that rhythm again.

Some time later she faltered again

and he knew it couldn't be done. He couldn't maintain this pace for another ten minutes, let alone two hours.

The knowledge settled on him like a great weight. He had no choice but to change his plan.

If he couldn't outrun them, then he'd need to hide. He couldn't ambush them. Not with just Plymouth's revolver. He had a rifle back at Kasey's but hadn't had time to collect it when he'd been running and hiding from Cowmeadow last night.

Running and hiding.

He sighed. Here he was doing exactly the same thing again. He just hoped he'd bought Plymouth enough time to get out of town unseen. At least then, whatever happened here, Luther Curry's death might not be in vain.

Hell, he didn't intend to die. He cut to the left, picking up a grassy trail that wound downwards to another dry riverbed. He slowed now, looking for a place to hide, looking for cover, looking for somewhere in which he would at least be protected for as long as possible. Maybe even somewhere they'd miss altogether.

But time and landscape were against him.

There was nothing but grass, rocks, dust, and openness.

★　★　★

'He was in the army,' Plymouth said. 'Not a lot of people round here know that.'

'The army? My, he is full of surprises.'

'He fought in the war.'

'The war?'

'The Mexican war.'

'I . . . I never thought of him as a soldier.'

'I'm not sure he was a very good one. But he joined up because he believed in . . . well, I'm not sure what Buzzard believed in. He was just a kid looking for adventure.'

'A soldier,' she said, thoughtfully.

Plymouth glanced across at her. He

smiled to himself. She was looking away to the left, watching the plain roll slowly beneath their wheels, her teeth gently biting down on her bottom lip.

'I'm not sure how much action he saw,' Plymouth said. 'I think he was there when they took Mexico City. But how much fighting he did, I've no idea. I think he went home soon after. Not sure soldiering was for him. I know he's a . . . '

'He's a what, Plymouth?'

'I don't know. Maybe a pacifist. You see a war, maybe it changes you. He's never one for carrying a gun and trying to be . . . a threat.'

She thought about this. Then said, 'You said he went home. Where was home?'

'Chicago, I believe. At least, somewhere in Illinois. He worked with ships, I believe.'

'He's full of surprises.'

'He keeps himself to himself, most of the time.'

'So I gather.'

From behind them the crack of a whip carried forward on the wind. They both turned. Someone in a wagon was approaching fast.

'It's Lloyd,' Mary Colton said. 'Lloyd Avery.'

★ ★ ★

The cave was barely more than a hollow in the side of the dry riverbank. The hollow was half covered by the huge roots of a tree that grew out over the riverbank and reached down into the earth like a great claw. Rocks and mud and weed had gathered in those roots.

It wasn't much. It wasn't enough. Buzzard knew enough about military strategy to understand that he needed to be on the high ground defending an impenetrable position, not backed into a corner such as this.

But there was no high ground. Not for fifty miles. And this was the only place he'd seen in fifteen minutes that offered any chance at all.

He rode to the edge of the hollow, jumped off his horse, and led her inside.

★ ★ ★

Sheldon Molloy said, 'Father, you'll have a drink, yes? To pay your respects. To celebrate Luther's life.'

Father Wiseman was staring down the road. There was still dust in the air from Lloyd Avery's wagon. 'Maybe I'll have a quick one.'

'That's the spirit, Father,' Molloy said. 'I was beginning to think everyone was leaving town. It's plumb the craziest funeral I've ever been to.'

Wiseman turned to him.

'You mean John Cowmeadow shooting at Buzzard Jones.'

'That was a bit . . . unexpected.'

'A trifle disrespectful,' Wiseman said. 'But I suspect John had good reason.'

'And to have his riders chasing Buzzard down? They were already in town. Waiting.'

'I don't know about that,' Wiseman said, his voice flat and emotionless as if the funeral service had taken all the feeling out of him.

'And everyone else? You think they were all put off by the shooting?'

'Everyone else? How do you mean?'

'I mean, look around you.'

He watched Wiseman's eyes do a slow circuit of the saloon. There was Jackson Arnold, Rodney Purse, Bill Carson and Gunther Krug leaning against the bar, already on their fourth whiskeys, still toasting Luther Curry. Jasper Owen and a couple of old-timers — August LeBlanc and Henry Williams — were sat at the window table. They'd been at the service, but not the burial. At the far end of the counter Penny Edward, who used to run a ferry on the Missouri but was now helping put up the new hotel and drinking everything he earned, and Crazy Clarence Cooder who, so far as Molloy knew did nothing, but always had half a dollar to spend on beer. The two of them were arguing over whose turn it was to buy the next drink. And sat at the piano, fingers quietly picking out a melancholy tune, probably from the old world, was Otto Wilhelm.

'I'm not familiar with your clientele,' Wiseman said. 'Is this not busy?'

'Sure it's busy,' Molloy said. 'But it's not busy with who I would have expected. Not today. Those boys at the bar excepting.'

'You were expecting . . . ?'

'More of the fellows from the burial, for one thing. I thought they'd have been back here to pay their last respects.'

'Well, John aside. I know Lloyd Avery had to make a start for Missouri.'

Molloy nodded. 'Fair enough. I thought Plymouth King might even have appeared for a drink. If only to calm his nerves after the shooting.'

'He's a friend of Buzzard's, yes?'

'Uh-huh. But he's lit out, too.'

'Plymouth King?'

'Uh-huh. Came down the hill, changed out of his best suit into his second best suit and headed out again. Him and Mary Colton.'

'Mary Colton was riding with Plymouth King?'

'Sure they were. See what I mean? Just about everybody I thought might join me for a drink is leaving town in a hurry.'

Clarence Cooder called along the bar. 'Hey, Moll. How about some service along here?'

'Bear with me a moment,' Molloy said to Father Wiseman. 'Let me serve the boys and then you and me can toast Luther properly.'

Molloy drew two more beers for Clarence Cooder and Penny Edward, and another round of whiskeys for Jackson, Rodney, Bill and Gunther. But when he came back to the end of the bar Father Wiseman was gone.

★ ★ ★

Buzzard Jones saw the first two riders gallop past the half-hidden hollow, neckerchiefs pulled high up over their faces to keep the dust from their mouths and noses. But the third rider happen to glance left, started to rein his horse up, then had second thoughts and let her run forward again. Buzzard counted five men before John Cowmeadow came by. None of them seemed to be riding as quickly as he had been, but he knew they would have ridden him down very soon. Their horses were wet and shiny with sweat, but the fact that there were so many of them must have made it easier.

After Cowmeadow had passed Buzzard remained motionless. The air in the gully was thick with dust. There was no breeze to blow it away. He wanted to wipe his face, try and get the grit out of his eyes. But he knew silence and stillness were the only allies he had.

They came back.

The one who had spotted something, a guy who looked a little like a

Mexican, must have signalled them to slow down. They returned slowly, quietly. They had rifles drawn. They formed a semicircle around the hollow, staring into the dark interior, the blazing sun making the shadows deeper.

'You gonna come out, Jones,' Cowmeadow said. 'Or we going to kill you in your hole like a rat?'

Somebody worked the lever on a rifle.

Buzzard stared at the men from his hiding place on the far side of the dry river bed. All he could see was the rear of the riders. He'd tied his horse up in the hollow and scampered back across the gully, and taken refuge behind some rocks on the far side. If he'd been prepared to shoot a man in the back he figured he could probably take one or two, maybe three of them, before they found their own cover.

It was tempting.

He thought back to a time, many years before, when he'd been killing men from the safety of the high rocks. At the time it had been war. He'd been under orders. Herb — whom he'd been aiming for this afternoon, and whom it looked as though he might never see again — had gloried in such activities. But it had never sat easy with Buzzard.

Still, looking at the men's backs, picturing what they'd done to Luther . . . imagining what they could do to *him,* it was tempting.

But it was not only cowardly. It was a death warrant. He looked over his shoulder. It was only a few feet to the top of the rise. If they started shooting he could probably slip up there and out of sight.

But what then?

Run the rest of the way on his bruised and battered legs?

It was all about buying time now. Whatever he chose to do, it was about giving Plymouth the biggest chance.

Someone pulled a revolver from a holster, fired a shot into the air.

Buzzard's horse whinnied and edged backwards out of the hollow a few steps.

'You walk on out with your hands up,' Cowmeadow said.

Buzzard aimed his own pistol at Cowmeadow's spine.

'Behind you,' he said.

Cowmeadow looked over his shoulder, yanked the reins of his horse and turned it around. The rider with the revolver already drawn half turned and fired a wild shot in the general direction of Buzzard, splintering a rock twenty yards to Buzzard's right. One of the other riders leaned way over his horse's neck, shielding his own body. Another turned slowly, pulling down the neckerchief that had been keeping the dust out of his nose and mouth, and in that moment Buzzard realized how wrong he'd been about absolutely everything.

10

Lloyd Avery said, 'Mary. What on earth . . . Where are you going?'

Plymouth eased his wagon to a halt. Lloyd pulled alongside. He sat upright on the bench at the front of his wagon.

'I needed to get away,' she said. 'Everything . . . you know . . . Luther.' She looked across at Plymouth and smiled, then turned back to Lloyd. 'Plymouth was heading east. He said I could ride along with him.'

'Whereabouts east?' Lloyd said to Plymouth. 'I've been trying to catch you. Two wagons travelling together are always better than one.'

Plymouth said, 'Cyprus Springs, by way of South Bottom. I need some wood and fittings.'

'I'll ride with you. I'm going through the crossing.' Lloyd looked at Mary. Plymouth wasn't sure whether something had passed between them. If there was more in Lloyd's self-invitation than pure companionship. 'I saw you at the church, Mary. But you didn't come up to the burial.'

'I intended to, but . . . ' She shook her head.

'I understand. It was a tough day.' Lloyd was already unwrapping the makings, his hands working seemingly of their own accord. Fingers pulled tobacco strands together and rolled paper whilst he talked.

'Funerals are never good,' Plymouth said.

'You saw him?' Lloyd Avery asked. 'I mean, when they brought him in?'

Plymouth glanced quickly at Mary, then across to Lloyd.

'Yeah, I saw him. It wasn't pretty.'

'Of course you did.' Lloyd nodded, looked down at the cigarette he was working on, nodded again and slipped it behind his right ear. 'Let me make up one more, then we'll get going again. No rush, hey?'

'No, no rush,' Plymouth said, looking up at the sun, seeing the way it had tracked way across the sky since they'd buried Luther Curry. They were going to have to make good time if they were to get to the crossing in time to find whoever was there.

And now, somehow, they were going to have to lose Lloyd Avery.

★ ★ ★

What he could see changed everything. For a moment he couldn't work it out. The heat and the brightness, the surprise, the thirst and the pain. It all mixed up inside his head and made it impossible to think. All he knew was that he had to explain his position very quickly if he wanted to live.

Buzzard said, 'I'm throwing my gun out. I could've shot any one of you but I didn't. Hold your fire.'

Just for a moment he hesitated, wondering whether these were to be the last moments of his life. Then he gently lobbed Plymouth's Colt out from behind the rock on to the gravely slope.

He raised his hands.

He slowly stood up.

* * *

Mary Colton whispered, 'Lloyd's all right, Plymouth. He's one of us.'

'What do you mean, us?'

'I mean . . . he's an abolitionist. He's part of the underground.'

'The same underground John Cowmeadow is part of?'

The wagon rocked as they rolled on, the wheels jarring in the deep ruts that had been cut into the hard ground over countless years by wagon trains working their way west from Missouri and often, as was the case now, back again.

'I still don't believe it,' she said.

'It seemed pretty cut and dried to me. I saw what they did to him last night.'

'He was looking black and blue when I saw him. But . . . '

'But what?'

'There's something not a lot of people know about John Cowmeadow. Something he doesn't talk about much in town.'

'What's that?' Plymouth said, looking across at her.

★ ★ ★

The bullet caught Buzzard in the left shoulder, spun him round and sent him sprawling to the ground. The base of his spine smashed into a rock and for a moment that pain was worse than the pain from the bullet.

Somebody said something, but he couldn't make out the words. The gunshot had left his ears ringing. A shadow fell over him — Cowmeadow on his horse, looking impossibly huge, a great silhouette.

'Time to talk,' Cowmeadow said.

Buzzard pressed a hand against his shoulder. It felt as if he'd been kicked. His right hand came away wet with blood and he could feel the muscles in his shoulder throbbing. His left hand was trembling uncontrollably. His arm was feeling warm, as if he was standing too close to a fire. He guessed the warmth would soon become a blazing heat.

'I had my hands up,' Buzzard said. He pressed his hand against the wound again, trying to keep the pain in, trying to keep his body together. He could smell powder and smoke. And he couldn't help but think of Luther Curry now. Tortured to death. But surely not by these men.

'You did? We must have missed that,' Cowmeadow said.

Now another shadow fell over Buzzard. He twisted slightly, the pain in his shoulder suddenly changing from that of a kick to feeling as if a knife had been plunged into his flesh.

One of Cowmeadow's men — a man with a straggly grey beard and a dirty brown jacket — was standing beside him, a rifle pointing down at Buzzard.

'John's got some questions for you,' the man said, and forced his rifle barrel between the fingers of Buzzard's right hand and into the fresh bullet wound.

Buzzard screamed.

He felt the world fade in and out of focus. His belly convulsed, and he twisted around trying to get away from the agony.

The man eased the rifle from the wound.

'You want to tell us what Luther Curry told you and your bastard friends now?' Cowmeadow said.

Buzzard said, 'You . . . you have . . . '

'Spit it out, boy,' the man in brown said.

'*You have black riders*,' Buzzard said. The man alongside Cowmeadow, also silhouetted now, but whom Buzzard had seen pull his neckerchief down just a few moments ago, was a Negro.

'We've got what?'

'You've got . . . black riders.'

In fact, Buzzard saw, there were two. One of the riders over to the right of

159

Cowmeadow, not directly in front of the sun, was a black man too. He sat on his horse looking tall and lean, his face the colour of wet coal.

The man jabbed his rifle into Buzzard's wound again. The pain exploded out of his shoulder in waves of fire. The whole world became orange and red and white. It felt as though Buzzard's brain was being torn in two.

'You don't like that, huh?' Cowmeadow was saying. 'You don't approve.'

'No . . . I mean . . . I thought.' It was impossible to form words. All he wanted to do was to be sick and then curl into a ball.

'You're an evil son-of-a-bitch,' Cowmeadow said. 'We should kill you right now.'

The man moved the barrel of his rifle from Buzzard's shoulder to his forehead.

'Wait!' Buzzard said.

'You going to beg? It'll be fun to watch but it won't stop us killing you. What you did to Luther . . . maybe we

160

should take your eyes first.'

'I didn't do that,' Buzzard said. 'For God's sake. I'm on your side!'

★ ★ ★

'He employs black men?' Plymouth said. 'Black cowboys?'

'On his range,' Mary Colton said. 'When it comes to abolition he seems to stand head and shoulders above any man I know. That's why so many people hate him. But he doesn't give a damn. 'If a man's free,' he says, 'then he's free to work for me.''

'Slaves?' Plymouth said.

'No. Free men. They were slaves once upon a time.'

'Then . . . '

'The more I think about it, the harder it is to believe,' Mary said.

'You don't think it's John?'

'I don't know whether it's *anybody*. I don't know whether Buzzard even heard right. There are a hundred people in town that shouldn't be trusted. John

Cowmeadow might be amongst them. But not on the issue of slavery.'

'So why is he after Buzzard?'

'Buzzard says it's because he beat John in a fight. Made him look bad. That would rile up John something terrible.'

'No. Buzzard figured it was because John wanted to stop him acting on what Luther had told him. This was the *one*, apparently.'

'Yes, Luther told us that, too.'

'Us?'

'Me. John. Lloyd. Father Wiseman. The underground.'

'Buzzard wanted to do it all alone.'

'Wanted to be a hero,' Mary said.

'Not quite. I think he was driven to it by guilt.'

'Guilt?'

'Yeah, he . . . well, it doesn't matter. He figured he didn't act honourably — '

'The boots.'

'You know about them?'

'John figured out there was something about them. Something about the timing. Buzzard told me earlier that Luther was still alive when he found him. But then . . . after they'd spoken, after Luther had died, your friend Buzzard took his boots and sold them.'

Plymouth nodded.

'That's about it.'

'And then he felt guilty.'

'Well, then your friend John Cow-meadow took him out into the middle of nowhere, and — excuse my language — beat the hell out of him trying to find out what Luther had told him.'

'And Buzzard didn't tell?'

'Nope. He figured the least he could do was to make good on Luther Curry's last request.'

'And because John beat him up he figured John was the enemy.'

'Maybe he is,' Plymouth said.

'No. There isn't an enemy. Not in our group. The enemy is all over town. All over east and south Kansas territory. All over Missouri. But it isn't any of us.'

He looked at her and shook his head. 'I'm so confused I'm even wondering whether or not I can trust you.'

'Of course you can, Plymouth,' she said. 'South Bottom, you mentioned earlier. Midnight. You'd better work this horse of yours a bit.'

* * *

The man with the beard had the barrel of his rifle resting on Buzzard's wounded shoulder again. The ground around Buzzard's left side was stained red, the dust congealing with blood and drying almost immediately in the sun.

'Guess you'd better talk,' John Cowmeadow said. 'And it better be pretty damn convincing or what you — or whoever — did to Luther'll be nothing compared to what we do to you.'

Buzzard glanced from John Cowmeadow across to one of his black skinned riders. Then he looked back at Cowmeadow.

'I thought you were pro-slavery,' he said.

'Does it look like it?'

'Luther Curry told me something before he died.'

'I figured as much.'

'But he told me not to trust anyone.'

'Yeah, Luther was a little careful like that. Too careful. Sometimes you have to be bold.'

'So I figured I try and do it alone.'

'Do what alone?'

'Bring 'em over.'

'Bring who over?' Cowmeadow said.

'The ones Luther Curry had lined up.'

'You know where and when?'

'Uh-huh. And I'd have done it, too, except you and your boys put a sack over my head and beat me.'

The bearded man glanced at the Mexican.

'You just trying to save your skin?' Cowmeadow said.

'I could have shot you back there,' Buzzard said.

'Yeah, but you couldn't have shot us all.'

'Maybe. Maybe not.'

'So tell me,' Cowmeadow said. 'Who are these people? And when and where are they going to be?'

'I don't know who they are. But they're going to be at South Bottom Crossing on the Black River at midnight. I was meant to take them up to Romego.'

'Jesus Christ,' Cowmeadow said. He raised a fist as if he wanted to punch the sky in anger. 'You've brought us four hours in the wrong direction. Jesus! The horses are exhausted.'

Buzzard stared up at him. The man's anger wasn't directed at Buzzard, just at the situation — at being fooled.

'It's OK,' Buzzard said. 'It's in hand.'

'How?'

'Plymouth King has gone. That's why I led you west. Give Plymouth time to get there.'

Cowmeadow looked down at him. He was silent for a few seconds.

'So you rode out here, figuring that we'd eventually capture and probably kill you, just to buy some time for Plymouth to rescue some black folks you don't even know?'

Buzzard nodded.

'Something like that.'

Cowmeadow looked over at one of his black riders. The man's expression never changed, although Plymouth saw Cowmeadow nodding slightly.

Cowmeadow looked back at him.

'And Plymouth, is he on his own.'

'Yeah.'

'And you trust him?'

'As the day is long.'

Cowmeadow jerked his head at the man with the rifle. He stepped backwards. Cowmeadow climbed down off his horse and held out his hand.

'I guess I owe you an apology. We need to get you back to town and get that shoulder looked at. How is it?'

'It hurts. But I'll live.'

Buzzard held on to Cowmeadow's hand and pulled himself upright. Inside, his body burned from the pain of the movement. It felt as though every muscle had been scorched.

'We ain't got time to work our way over to the South Bottom,' one of the black men said. 'What we gonna do?'

'Plymouth's a good man,' Buzzard said.

'Luther Curry said this was to be the *one*,' another said. 'We don't want to risk losing them.'

'Then head for Romego,' Buzzard said. 'That's where they'll be going.'

'Maybe the road to Romego?' Cowmeadow said. 'Join up with them heading north. Protect them from there on in.'

Cowmeadow looked at Buzzard.

'Your shoulder OK with that?'

'Uh-huh.'

'Sure?'

'Yep.'

'Then let's go and free some more slaves.'

11

Plymouth King and Mary Colton pulled into South Bottom Crossing at 10.30. Lloyd Avery was right on their tail. The moon, just a day into the waning phase, gave everything a clean look. The town, on the edge of the river, and at a place where several trails converged, was older, more mature, and more defined than New Whitby. As they rode into town they passed large wooden and brick homes behind white picket fences. Then, a little further on, stood less ornate and simpler buildings with huge fenced-off corrals, most of them empty at the moment, just a few with small herds of longhorns and a few horses in them. Further in, there were more shops and businesses — a watchmaker's and a barber's, a dentist and a general store, a sheriff's office and a livery stable, a hardware store and a jeweller's. Several of them had outside steps leading up to second storeys. The plankwalk was higher and more complete than New Whitby's. Several side roads ran off the main road at right angles. Oil lamps and candles burned in numerous windows, and they saw at least three saloons from which the sound of laughter and music and raised voices could be heard. The air smelled of animals, water, and manure, and the dust that they were all so used to in Whitby was only noticeable by its absence. In the heart of the town the buildings looked squeezed together, standing side by side with the plankwalk connecting them and, at one point, on one side of the street, wooden pillars supported a long roof above the walk for maybe fifty yards. Horses were hitched to railings outside the saloons and the sheriff's office, a few people wandered around taking no notice of the wagons passing through. Some folks sat on rocking-chairs out

front of their properties and watched the strangers unconcernedly. A church, far bigger than Whitby's, rose up in silhouette from one of the side streets.

'You forget how small our town is, don't you?' Plymouth said.

Mary Colton, Plymouth's blanket wrapped around her shoulders, was looking from one side of the street to the other. A dog had come from somewhere and was trotting alongside them. They passed several water troughs in the centre of town. Plymouth steered his horse over to one of them, letting the animal drink.

'It's grown a little since I last came through,' Mary said.

Lloyd Avery stopped his wagon for his horse to drink and walked across, standing beside Plymouth.

'You stopping here?' he said. 'For the night?'

Mary Colton looked at Plymouth. He glanced at her, then looked down at Lloyd. Lloyd was just lighting up a cigarette.

'What is it?' Lloyd said.

Mary had sworn to Plymouth that Lloyd could be trusted. For an hour they'd argued the case, whispering back and forth. Plymouth had been unmoving on his decision to do this alone. 'Then how are you going to get rid of Lloyd?' she'd said.

'Do you know where you're looking?' Mary said to Plymouth now. 'It's a big town.'

Plymouth glared at her.

'What are you looking for?' Lloyd said. 'We passed a hotel back . . . ' He let the words die. 'This is it, isn't it?' he said, breathing out a cloud of smoke. 'You're here because of Luther, aren't you?'

Plymouth said, 'I have no idea what you're talking about.'

Lloyd took a long pull on his cigarette.

Mary said, 'Oh for goodness' sake. Plymouth, look at this place.' She swept her left hand out across in front of her.

'What?' Plymouth said.

172

'Do you know where you're going? I mean, do you know where to go now?'

It had already crossed his mind several times, a dozen times even. And the closer he'd come to the river crossing town the more insistent the question had become. He knew how big the place was. A man could find a hundred places to hide. A thousand even. Even before he'd set off, when talking to Buzzard, he'd known that there would be this problem. But he'd figured it would sort itself out. So long as he put himself in the right place at the right time things would work out. A man had to have faith.

Lloyd let the smoke stream from his mouth.

'Me and Mary,' he said, 'we've been here before. A couple of times. You know what I mean when I say that?'

Plymouth looked down at him.

'It was a while back,' Lloyd said. 'When we first started bringing them across. But I guess ol' Luther might be using the same place again.'

'You know where they'll be?' Plymouth said.

'You trust me?'

'It seems I have no choice.' Maybe faith was repaying his trust, just not in the way he had expected.

'It's too late anyway,' Lloyd said. 'Now we're here you'd better hope I'm on the same side as . . . '

'Me,' Plymouth said.

'I was going to say, God.'

Plymouth nodded, then he smiled. 'It's the same thing,' he said. 'Where are we going, then?'

'Cross the river,' Lloyd said. 'Ain't no slaves going to risk coming over on the ferry on their own.'

Plymouth looked between the dark shapes of the buildings — some of them large storehouses — that lined the street down to the silver strip of water. The river here was not vast, but it was too deep and too wide for horses, and crossing with wagons would be impossible.

'Does the ferry run at night?'

'Uh-huh. If you've got the money then Tommy's got the muscles.'

They rode down to the water's edge. The ferry was pulled close up against the riverbank, its rope tight around a tree stump. A second ferry, larger, was in the process of being constructed, its wooden framework looking like the skeleton of a great animal from eons before. The ferry keeper's hut was off to one side of the road; a faint line of light came from beneath the door and round the edges of the curtains covering the small window. Lloyd climbed off his wagon and banged on the cabin door. It opened immediately. The man — Tommy, Plymouth assumed — stood there with an oil lamp in one hand and gun in the other. Plymouth recalled being hauled across the river several times by the man, without ever learning his name. Each time the man had been drunk, but he'd always taken Plymouth across swiftly and safely.

'Choo want?' Tommy said, lifting the lamp higher, getting a good look at

Lloyd. 'I seen you before.'

'We want to cross,' Lloyd said.

Tommy looked beyond Lloyd and saw Mary and Plymouth.

'Pretty one,' Tommy said.

'How much is a crossing?'

'Can't take both wagons together. It'll be two crossings. That'll be two dollars.'

'Two dollars?'

'It's late. You woke me.'

'You must be the richest man in South Bottom.'

'Take it or leave it.'

'We want to come back, too.' Plymouth said.

Tommy looked at him.

'What?'

'We want you to wait for us on the other side.'

'You want me to haul you over one at a time and then haul you back?'

'Yes.'

Tommy looked from Lloyd to Plymouth and then to Mary. His eyes stayed on Mary the longest. Then he looked back at Lloyd and said, 'Ferry's closed. Sorry, fellows.'

He stepped back inside the cabin and slammed the door.

'What you go and say that for?' Lloyd said.

'We have to get back over. We need to get to . . .'

'Get to where?' Lloyd said.

'Romego,' Mary said.

Lloyd stared at Plymouth.

'A man named Powder, I'll bet,' Lloyd said.

'You know?' Plymouth said.

'You should have trusted us from the beginning.'

'I'm sorry. Look, I have . . . ten dollars. Knock on his door, tell him we'll pay him ten dollars.'

'You're crazy,' Lloyd said. 'He'll do it for five. Hell, I'd do it for five.'

Tommy stood at the front of the ferry and hauled on the rope that pulled them across the river, the flow helping the crossing.

'I ain't saying nothing,' he said. 'But

the only folks want to go across and straight back again are either sightseers or they're bringing someone over they shouldn't be. And there ain't no sights worth seeing that side of the river.'

Later, when he'd gone back across the water and had brought Lloyd over, he said, 'I'm going back to my whiskey. You whistle when you're ready to come back. If I'm asleep you'll have to wait until morning.'

* * *

On the eastern side there were fewer buildings, but the town was still spreading away from the river. There were corrals and warehouses, a few bunkhouses, and a single saloon. The place felt darker, the buildings seemed even closer together than on the western side, if that was possible. This near to the river there was no one around. Plymouth could hear the low croak of frogs and smell the water, a breeze cooled his forehead. A bird flew low overhead and that made him think of Buzzard. Actually, Buzzard had been on his mind the whole journey. When he hadn't been concentrating on steering the wagon, hadn't been worrying about how he was going to lose Lloyd Avery when they all got to South Bottom, or wondering where on earth in the river-crossing town they were going to have to look to find the slaves; when he hadn't been cursing himself for trusting pretty Mary Colton — because, all through the journey, he couldn't help but wonder if he hadn't been tricked; when none of these thoughts were prominent there was always Buzzard. Buzzard somewhere back there in the territory riding for his life, riding for the lives of some slaves he'd never met. Had he made it? Did he get to Herb's ranch or had they run him down somewhere along the trail? Plymouth liked Buzzard. Maybe he'd even consider him a friend, though Buzzard had always seemed a bit of loner. But these last few days there'd been a change in Buzzard. He had never been selfish, but now . . . now he seemed self*less*. And Plymouth couldn't help but think that fate often waited until a man changed for the better before dealing him the worst hand of cards.

Along the river front there were wooden jetties built out into the river, wooden sheds built at the rear of the jetties. Rats scurried away from them. Something splashed in the water, rippling the reflection of the moon.

'You know where you're going?' Plymouth said to Lloyd.

'I know where I went last time. Wait here.'

★ ★ ★

Mary Colton said, 'I'm sorry I gave it away to Lloyd. I knew he could be trusted.'

Plymouth sighed. 'It's all right. It's worked out. I was a bit angry for a moment back there, but — '

Across the river a horse whinnied. Voices were carried to them on the breeze.

Plymouth twisted around on the wagon bench. There were four — no, five — men on horses at the ferry landing. Plymouth's heart raced. He felt a trembling in his belly. The town was quiet, save for the saloons. The trail had been empty except for their two wagons.

It didn't feel right.

He and Mary were parked in the deep shadows of a riverside warehouse. But they weren't hidden. Any great movement, or if the men across the river just stared long and hard enough, they'd be seen. That was assuming that the men were looking for them.

It was an assumption that Plymouth made.

Why else would five men have turned up on the western side of South Bottom and, instead of riding straight to a saloon to quench whatever thirst they had, head straight down to the crossing?

As Plymouth watched, one of them

jumped off his horse and went to rap on Tommy's door.

Tommy opened the door. This time he had the oil lamp in one hand and a bottle of whiskey in the other. The man said something, Plymouth couldn't make the words out. He saw Tommy shake his head. The man said something else, and this time Tommy paused, stepped out of the cabin and looked across the river. Then he pointed directly at Plymouth and Mary.

'They've seen us,' Plymouth whispered.

'Do you think they're after us?'

'Do you want to take the chance?'

Across the river the man was hurrying Tommy on to his ferry. The other four horsemen rode on to the flat wooden deck, then Tommy reached up for the rope that hung all the way across the river and started hauling.

The men stared at Plymouth and Mary.

'I don't recognize any of them,' Plymouth said.

They were a quarter of the way

across the river now. One of the riders at the front of the ferry raised his hand. 'Evening,' he called.

'I gave Buzzard my gun,' Plymouth said.

'The second one on the left,' Mary said. 'You notice anything strange about him?'

Plymouth squinted into the darkness. 'Fellow with a beard. Looks like he's only got one arm.'

Suddenly Mary jumped down off the wagon.

'Mary!' Plymouth called, but she ignored him.

She ran across the street, the dirt hard-packed from all the wagons and horses and cattle that must have passed at this point. Plymouth watched her sprint to the landing-stage on this side of the river. The rope on which Tommy was hauling stretched above head-height across the landing-stage, and was tied around the cut-off trunk of what must have been a huge tree. Mary reached inside her dress and, to

Plymouth's amazement, pulled out a small pistol.

'Hey!' Tommy called. 'What choo doing? Stop that.'

One of the riders was quick to react. He pulled a revolver from his hip holster.

'Mary!' Plymouth yelled.

The rider fired his gun and a chunk of tree trunk exploded right beside Mary's head. For a moment Plymouth thought she'd been hit. She crouched behind the tree, and he saw her pull a small bag out of her dress.

Another bullet smashed into the tree.

She was pouring powder into the gun, now forcing a ball down the barrel, now trying to find something else in that bag.

Two of them had guns out now. Bullets slammed into the tree.

Then she stood up and reached round the tree, pressing the barrel of her Derringer against the rope and pulled the trigger.

Plymouth waited for the misfire. He

didn't know much about Derringers but he knew they were forever misfiring, sometimes even exploding. He didn't hear the gun go off, but then she jumped to the ground — at least, he prayed she'd jumped, rather than been hit.

'Sonofabitch!' Tommy cried, as the rope he was hauling on went slack and the river current started pulling the ferry downstream.

All the riders were firing now. Two with handguns, three with rifles. Plymouth curled as low as he could in the front of the wagon. The last thing he saw was Mary diving to the ground behind the big tree trunk, and the ferry going downstream, being pulled towards the far bank by the rope that Tommy still held, which was now only connected to the far side of the river.

Still crouching down, Plymouth said 'Git on gone' and moved the wagon out, working his way blindly to where Mary was.

Bullets were still whistling all around

them, some thumping into wooden buildings, others disappearing into the night. One buried itself into the back of the wagon seat and Plymouth felt a punch in his right buttock. On both sides of the river doors were opening, people were coming out of buildings cautiously.

Plymouth heard someone shout, 'What's going on? Is it the Yankees?'

'Get behind the horse,' he whispered to Mary.

She stood up. There was a patch of blood on her face. It looked black in the darkness. He turned the wagon and started moving away from the river, Mary keeping the horse between her and the gunshots.

'Where's Lloyd?' she said.

'You're crazy,' Plymouth said. He found he wasn't scared. He was excited. He felt like laughing. Giggling hysterically, even.

'What's going on, partner,' someone said, stepping out into the street. He had a gun in his hand and was vaguely swinging it in Plymouth's direction. Maybe, Plymouth figured, the fellow thinks that if all these people are shooting at me then he should as well. Maybe he thought there might be money on my head.

'Fellow across the river,' Plymouth said. 'I'm afraid I just stole his wife.'

'What?'

Mary Colton said, 'He's lying. He didn't *steal* me. I came willingly. But my goddamn husband ain't happy and wants to kill us both.'

A bullet from across the river hit the back of Plymouth's wagon, and ricocheted into the man's arm.

'Sonofabitch,' he said, and turned and started firing across the water.

Plymouth urged his horse on.

More people were coming out on to the street. Plymouth heard someone say 'Fellow there's run off with someone's wife.'

Somebody said, 'He can run off with mine, too, if he wants.'

The shooting was more sporadic

now. The men across the river had maybe realized that Plymouth had slipped behind cover and that anyone they might hit would be more trouble than they needed. Furthermore, people were firing back on them. Plymouth wasn't experienced in such things but figured that that would probably make a man think twice.

A woman leaning out of an upstairs window said, 'I ain't heard so much lead being flung around since some blacks tried to escape up North.'

'We hung them fellows good, didn't we, Agnes?' someone said from the doorway below her.

'We sure did. Ain't no slaves slipping away through our town.'

Just then, Lloyd Avery drove his wagon round the corner. Three people were sitting in the back behind him.

12

Buzzard said, 'You guys go on without me.'

His shoulder felt as though it were on fire. They'd dressed the wound as best they could, tearing Buzzard's under-shirt into two pieces, packing one piece against each side of his shoulder and then holding it in place with his belt, running it across his left shoulder, under his right armpit, and pulling as tightly as they could. The pain was bad enough when he was motionless, but it was unbearable when they were push-ing the horses on.

The way they'd figured it, they'd head north-east, looking to join the trail to Romego at Thirty Mile Ridge a few hours north of South Bottom. Unless Plymouth had swapped out his old horse for Lady Suffolk then, guaran-teed, they'd be ahead of him.

But anything more than walking pace was killing Buzzard, and he knew he was slowing them down terribly.

John Cowmeadow brought his horse alongside Buzzard. For a moment he didn't speak. Then he said, 'Is it still bleeding?'

'Maybe a little,' Buzzard said, pressing his right hand against the blood-soaked shirt. 'It's hard to tell.'

'You ain't going to die,' Cowmeadow said. 'I've seen a lot of men shot in the arm. It's not like being shot in the thigh or the belly.'

'I'm not worried about dying, just about slowing you down.'

Cowmeadow nodded.

'You get on back to Whitby. Blue, you stay with Buzzard here, make sure he don't pass out.'

'I'm OK,' Buzzard said. 'I want to head up to Romego. I started this. I want to see it through.'

Cowmeadow nodded again.

'I understand. If you're sure. It's further to Romego than — '

'I'm sure.'

'OK. Blue will make sure you're OK. I'll make sure your slaves are waiting to thank you.'

Now it was Buzzard's turn to nod.

Cowmeadow smiled, then turned his horse and, with the rest of his men except Blue, they spurred their horses on and away.

★ ★ ★

At some point Buzzard fell asleep on his horse. The sun had gone down and the stars and the moon were slowly gaining in strength. The landscape had turned black and white and grey and his shoulder, no longer being hammered with every horse step, had gone numb. Blue had pulled out a small bottle of whiskey once the other guys had gone out of sight. He'd offered most of it to Buzzard. They'd talked for a while, Blue telling Buzzard about how much John Cowmeadow did to bring slaves over from Missouri and into freedom. Buzzard told Blue about finding Luther Curry. He told Blue about the Mexican war and Blue told him about a gunfight he'd once been in back in Fort Scott.

Blue asked Buzzard if he had a woman and Buzzard had said no, but a picture of Mary Colton had formed in his mind. Blue said he had a wife and a daughter back across the river in Arkansas but he hadn't seen them in a year. He was still trying to make enough money to buy some land and bring them across.

They talked about the river and the best places to cross, about the best way to cook rabbit, and the best run of cards they'd ever been dealt in games of poker and faro. They talked about guns they'd owned or heard about and they talked about horses they'd ridden. They talked about the cities back East they'd visited or lived in and they talked about Indians.

They smoked cigarettes that Blue rolled as they rode and Blue told

Buzzard the names of some of the stars they could see. Buzzard knew the stars anyway, but never said anything. They talked about the politics of slavery and about the last two presidents and they talked about the songs they knew — though neither was prepared to sing — and they talked about the new businesses springing up in Whitby and how a man could make a lot of money if he could just get started.

At some point Buzzard's chin dropped to his chest and his eyes closed and a peace came over him from all the pain of the last two days, and although he was aware of the slow movement of his horse, it was a dreamlike knowledge and time passed without him realizing.

The gunshot woke him.

He was disorientated. Where was he? Why was there a riderless horse alongside him?

Why was Father Wiseman pointing a rifle at him?

★ ★ ★

They tied his hands to the horn of his saddle, the rope short enough to force him to hunch forward, his injured shoulder on fire again.

'I sent a bunch of men after your friend Plymouth,' Wiseman said. 'My fastest riders. And me, Slim, and Scoop here, followed John Cowmeadow, who was following you.'

Buzzard gritted his teeth. He'd been kidnapped and beaten. He'd been shot and tortured. Now he was bound and in agony again. He thought back to Luther Curry. Maybe I'm ending up the same way as him, he thought. Except in instalments.

'Shame about your friend,' Wiseman said. 'Still, the birds will enjoy him.'

They left Blue lying in the dirt and followed the tracks left by the rest of John Cowmeadow's group as they rode towards the road to Romego.

'How can you do this?' Buzzard said, twisting his head so he could see Wiseman.

Wiseman looked across at him. His

eyes were bloodshot and tired. There were deep lines in his forehead.

'Do what, my friend?'

'You know what.'

Buzzard looked beyond Wiseman. Neither of his two riders — Slim or Scoop — was paying any attention to the bound man and the priest. Buzzard realized that Wiseman had quietly been doing exactly what John Cowmeadow had done — building a small army of private supporters that had always remained behind the scenes, but that now — because of whom Luther Curry had arranged to bring to freedom this time — had suddenly been forced into the open.

'Slavery?' Wiseman said.

'I thought you were on . . . on our side,' Buzzard said.

Wiseman smiled.

'I didn't know that you had a side.'

'I do now.'

'Shame you picked the wrong one, then.'

'Did you kill Luther Curry? I thought

he was one of your friends.'

'Luther was a good man. But he was getting a little . . . over zealous.'

'You killed him?'

'Not personally.'

Buzzard looked over at the other riders. They were barely more than black shapes in the moonlight. Were these the men? Were they the brutal torturers who had scooped a man's eyes out and left him hanging to die. *Scooped.* Jesus. He shuddered and the movement brought fresh pain bursting from his shoulder.

'I thought a man of the cloth . . . '

Buzzard's horse stumbled and he gasped in pain as the shock waves ran all the way up his arm. Even though the pace was slow the horse was close to exhaustion.

'I gather you don't read the Bible,' Wiseman said, the moonlight catching him just so and illuminating half his face with yellow light. The other half was in shadow. He looked like the Devil, Buzzard thought. Wiseman laughed. 'Sorry,

I was assuming you could read.'

'I can read.'

'Then look up Leviticus. Chapter 25. 'Your male and female slaves are to come from the nations around you; from them you may buy slaves. You can will them to your children as inherited property and can make them slaves for life.'

'Or if that's not clear enough for you, how about this from Genesis. From the very beginning of time, Mr Jones. 'If a man beats his male or female slave with a rod and the slave dies as a direct result, he must be punished, but he is not to be punished if the slave gets up after a day or two, since the slave is his property.' I'd say that's pretty clear, Mr Jones.'

'Then why have you been working with . . . with John and Mary and the others to — '

'To bring slaves to freedom?'

Buzzard looked over at the priest. 'Yes.'

Wiseman smiled again. 'Sometimes

small defeats can help win the war.'

'You let them think — '

'Yes, I let them think. Something they weren't very good at. I knew there would be a day like this one. A night like this one, when they might choose to do something that *could* make a difference. Let's be honest, everything else they've ever done, every individual slave they've *illegally* smuggled to freedom hasn't meant a thing — other than to the slave himself. I'm happy for them to do that. I'm happy to be involved. It meant that come a night like this . . . I'm ready.'

'What are you going to do?'

'It's already done, Mr Jones.'

'What?'

'My men will already have caught up with your friend. Maybe he'll be OK.' He shrugged. 'Maybe not. But the men that he had gone to save will be back where they belong. Either that or . . . ' Wiseman shrugged.

Buzzard felt a coldness grip his spine. He thought of Plymouth, the innocent man, not a soldier, not a fighter. But a good man. A man who hadn't deserved to be pulled into such a situation.

'So why are you here? Why did you follow John?'

'Loose ends, my friend. It's actually all your fault. Well, not quite. Without you picking the bones of the dead things would have carried on as normal. The slaves wouldn't have had a chance to get across and would have probably been captured by noon tomorrow as they wandered aimlessly around Missouri. But you and Plymouth gave them a chance. So I had to stop them. And, sadly, I need to stop you and John too. I assume — I need to assume — that you had me worked out.'

Buzzard said, 'We hadn't. We knew there was someone. We didn't know who.'

Father Wiseman nodded.

'Sadly — for you. Now you do know.'

13

Lloyd Avery said hurriedly, 'Don't say a word. I'll explain later. I gather we can't go back that way.'

'No.'

'Then let's head north.'

Plymouth looked at him, and then at the three people in the back of his wagon. There were two women and a man. All were dirty and wearing rags. Their cheeks were hollow and their eyes sunken. All three of them were white.

'Right behind you,' Plymouth said, and he pulled on his reins and turned in behind Lloyd.

Somebody called 'Good luck with the other fellow's wife.'

They drove through the outskirts of town, the sound of occasional gunfire in the distance. People were shouting and laughing behind them. Somewhere there was the tinkle of smashing glass.

On the eastern edge of South Bottom Crossing they turned off the main Missouri trail and started across country, northbound, on a track that looked as though it was seldom used. The moon illuminated ruts and boulders and clumps of grass and small bushes. Jack rabbits ran for cover.

After fifteen or twenty minutes they found themselves on flat grassland. A line of trees a mile to their left marked the course of the river. They could still smell the water in the air. The going became easier and Plymouth pulled alongside Lloyd.

'Well?' he said.

'What happened back there?' Lloyd said. 'I thought a war had started.'

'What happened was Mary saved our skins. She shot the ferry.'

'She shot the ferry?'

'I shot through the rope,' Mary said. 'There were a whole bunch of them coming for us.'

'I think I need a cigarette,' Lloyd said. He reached behind his ear. There wasn't one there. He turned to the white man in the back of his wagon. 'Jethro, can you take the reins?'

'Sure can.'

Plymouth saw the stubble on the man's face, the dirt ingrained into his forehead. The man climbed forward and sat on the bench alongside Lloyd. Lloyd pulled out the makings and started to roll a cigarette.

'Jethro?' Plymouth said.

'Uh-huh,' Jethro said.

'Plymouth King. Pleased to meet you.'

'This here is Josephine and her sister Louvain.'

'Pleased to meet you,' Plymouth said.

The women smiled. They looked scared, Plymouth thought. No, they looked terrified. The one called Josephine had long hair hanging over her face.

Mary said, 'Excuse me for stating the obvious, but — '

'We're white,' Josephine said.

'Yes. I was expecting — '

'You know nothing,' Jethro said. There was a cold anger in his voice.

Lloyd Avery placed a cigarette in the corner of his mouth, flicked a lucifer into life with his thumbnail, and lit up. Once he had the cigarette going he handed it to Jethro and set about rolling another.

'How do you know they were after us?' Jethro said to Mary. 'The ones across the river, I mean.'

'One of them had an arm missing.'

'Lots of folks got arms missing, miss,' Jethro said. He breathed out cigarette smoke.

'The last time I saw him . . . it was when he gave me a letter telling me where I'd find Luther's body,' she said. 'He was one of the ones who killed Luther.'

Josephine and Louvain both crossed themselves.

'You knew him?' Plymouth asked. 'Luther Curry, I mean.'

'I knew of him,' Josephine said. Louvain nodded. 'She doesn't speak,'

Josephine explained. 'They cut her tongue out.'

'Who did?' Mary asked.

'Who d'you think?' Jethro said. 'We called him 'Boss'.'

'Boss?'

'Lord help us,' Jethro said. 'We're slaves, miss. White slaves. You never heard of such things before?'

Jethro told them the story as they drove their wagons north towards the crossing at Black Rock Shallows, the only place for fifty miles they could cross the river back into Kansas territory with wagons.

They'd been living on a small settlement in a place called Freedom, Arkansas. Jethro said it had to be the most inappropriate place-name he'd ever heard. There were half a dozen families working the land. They had some cattle, some hens, half a dozen goats. The land was good but the work was hard. They were struggling but getting by. Slowly, very slowly, they were making a go of it. They helped each other. Building up cabins, destoning the land, ploughing, seeding, sowing, fencing. Even slaughtering. There were three children born in Freedom. It boded well for the future.

Then the lead men came.

Lead, as in the metal, Jethro said.

There were a dozen of them. Hats pulled low, neckerchiefs over their faces. They rode in with guns drawn. They set fire to the cabins. They dragged the men and the young women out and tied their hands, led them away, ropes around their necks.

'You didn't fight?' Lloyd said.

'Oh we fought all right,' Jethro said. 'They shot my brother Willis in the belly. He was lying screaming on the ground. They shot one of the babies. I had an old Sharps. I got one of them. Then they knocked me to the ground. One of them put a gun in my mouth, but another said no, don't kill him. It'll be worse for him alive. Then they raped my wife in front of me.'

Louvain made a sound. Plymouth

looked at her. Tears were rolling down her face.

'I had a knife,' Josephine said. 'I went for one of them. He took the knife off me and used it to cut my face.' She pulled her hair away from her face. There were scars on both sides of her face.

'They were right,' Jethro said. 'It was worse being alive. Every day . . . the memories . . . the not knowing. I never saw my wife again.'

'They took us to the mines,' Josephine said. 'The lead mines in south east Missouri. We weren't the only ones. The only whites, I mean. There were — there are — dozens and dozens.'

They told of the conditions underground, the darkness and the dust, the whipping, the prison they were kept in. They told of how one man, a white man, who tried to escape had the tendons in his ankles severed and was put on bellows duty from there on in. Others, Jethro said, who became too ill to work, were used for target practice.

'People knew about us,' Jethro said. 'They had to.'

'That's what we believed,' Josephine said. She was holding Louvain's hand. 'It was the only thing that kept us going. Someone somewhere must know and surely they'd do something about it.'

'And that someone was Luther,' Lloyd said.

'I never even knew his name,' Jethro said. 'Until you' — he nodded at Lloyd — 'came and found us in the cattle house down at the riverside.'

They never knew how Luther found out about them, or how he set up their escape. It was done through a man called Howarth. A black man, Jethro said. He never figured why Howarth didn't come with them.

'He told me the people still there needed him,' Josephine said. 'And that if we came West, and then North and told our story, then all of them would eventually be free.'

'Breaking out four nights ago was

one of the most terrifying things we've ever done,' Jethro said. 'When you've seen what they did to others. I mean . . . ' He looked at Louvain. 'All she did was complain once about not being able to have a drink.'

Louvain smiled sadly. She could be, Plymouth thought, a breathtakingly beautiful woman. Would be, once she'd been fed for a few months and had chance to clean up and cut off some of her matted hair. But would she ever recover inside?

'But we agreed we'd go for it. Or die trying,' Josephine said.

What happened, Jethro explained, was that four nights ago someone cut a hole in the wire fence.

'We slept down in the mine six nights a week, sometimes seven, but this was July the fourth. They said we could have the day off, you know, to show us how *wonderful* and *kind* they were.' He spat over the edge of the wagon. 'There was wine and some of the black slaves were playing some music. They were very good. A lot of them worked above ground so I guess they had time to practise. They liked to keep the whites out of sight.'

He sighed. 'I don't know — sometimes I wonder just who was involved. Whether it was one of the owners who was kind of sick of what was going on, how things had gotten so out of hand, maybe. I don't know. Part of me wants to believe that there's good even in those people — '

'There ain't,' Josephine said.

'Anyway, someone knew we'd be up that day and they got a message to me that if I really wanted to do this there'd be a gap in the wire and they'd set it up so we'd have time to get out unseen. I didn't know what they meant at the time. They also wanted me to bring someone else, some women, they said. I understood that there was politics behind this. But, hell, we just wanted out.'

'But I'd seen a man whipped just for holding on to the fence and looking out at freedom,' Josephine said. 'And I seen another have his — '

'What she's saying,' Jethro said, 'is that we knew that if we got caught it was going to be bad.'

Lloyd Avery stuck a new cigarette into his mouth and said, 'Son of a bitch. The world needs to know about all of this. No wonder they were so keen to stop Luther this time.'

'How did you manage it?' Mary said, holding on to the side of Plymouth's wagon as they hit a slight rise in the trail going north.

'There was an explosion,' Jethro said. 'A huge blast, way over by the boss's house. Gunfire, too. I don't know what it was, or how it happened. But it was big. Just about everyone was rushing over there. It was after dark. A lot of folk were drunk and confused.'

Josephine said, 'See, it was easy to get out. But there was nowhere to go. That's why they weren't worried. Anyone who got out would be hunted down in a day or less.'

'They had dogs,' Jethro said.

'And the punishments — we ain't told you a half of it,' Josephine said. 'Nobody would run, even if the whole fence was down.'

'Except we did,' Jethro said. 'It got to the point where somebody had to. 'Course we had help. They were waiting for us with horses. I've never ridden so fast. We were through that fence and gone. The next day we were holed up in the back of a stables someplace. I never saw it in the daylight. Next night some different folk brought us further west in a wagon like this. We were hidden beneath boxes.'

'We didn't actually know where we were going. North, west, east — I guessed we weren't going south,' Josephine said, squeezing Louvain's hand.

'Three days later, here we are,' Jethro said.

The moon had tracked far across the sky as Jethro and Josephine had told their story. A new day was starting to lighten the sky in the east.

'We can cut back across the river, just up here a piece,' Lloyd said. 'Maybe a few more hours. Once we get you up to Romego you'll be safe.'

Then Mary Colton said. 'There's someone on our tail. Coming fast.'

★　★　★

Dawn was breaking as John Cowmeadow's group eventually hit the road to Romego. They'd had to stop several times, even after they'd left Buzzard and Blue. The horses were simply too tired to keep on moving. A band of light blue was growing way across on the Missouri horizon, the sky suddenly seeming darker all around them because of that light. Trees and rocks, horses and riders started to have some detail upon their shapes.

John Cowmeadow's horse was suddenly a little more lively.

'The river's just over yonder,' he said. The thickening line of trees that grew beside the river was a mile away to the east. 'The horses can smell it.'

'I can smell it, too, boss,' one of the black riders — Washington — said.

The Mexican — Raul — was studying the ground.

'Ain't nobody been through here in weeks,' he said. 'We're ahead of them, boss. Look at this grass. Tough stuff. Ain't rained in months and it's still spreading like the pox.'

'Moisture in the air from the river,' Cowmeadow said. 'Come on, let's go and drink.'

★   ★   ★

The white slave, Jethro, yanked on the reins and yelled for the horse to hurry up, but she had nothing left. She kept going forward at a slow and steady rate. Louvain was making strange sounds from her tongueless mouth and Josephine had her arm wrapped around Louvain's shoulders. She was whispering something to her, telling her it was going to be all right, that they weren't going to go back to the mine. But as she said the words she was looking over her shoulder, her eyes wide open and terrified. Lloyd was digging around in the back of his wagon underneath a tarp. He came up with a shotgun.

Mary Colton looked from Lloyd's wagon back to the men chasing them down. It was the same men she'd set adrift in the river back at South Bottom. She was sure of that. Someone must have swum across the river with the rope and reattached it. The dust they were kicking up looked silver in the dawn light. There were five of them, spread across the trail. Two had rifles in their hands.

She dug her own tiny gun out from her dress and started trying to charge it again. It was hardly worth the effort, she thought, but what else could she do? Plymouth was leaning forward, urging his horse on. She recalled him saying that he'd given his gun to Buzzard.

'How far away are they?' he said breathlessly.

'Less than half a mile,' she said.

He threw a quick glance at her. He looked tired. He'd been driving the wagon all night. He'd been tricked and shot at and now he was being chased. He looked to be in pain, too. She wondered if one of the bullets back at South Bottom had actually hit him. 'Git on gone!' he called, but the horse never accelerated.

'Is that it?' he said.

She was trying to work a cartridge into the tiny barrel of the Derringer. The bouncing of the wagon made it almost impossible.

'Is what it?'

'That's all we've got to fight with?'

She saw Lloyd kneeling in the back of his wagon loading a shotgun.

'Just about,' she said.

'And there's five of them?'

She looked again. Two had peeled off very wide and were galloping away from the others.

'I think they're going to circle us,' she said.

Ahead of them Lloyd's wagon hit a ridge in the trail. She saw all of them — Lloyd and Josephine, Louvain and Jethro thrown upwards in their seats. For a second she thought Lloyd had lost the shotgun but he caught it.

A second later they hit the same ridge. She was thrown upwards too, and when she came back down the impact made her bite her tongue. She tasted blood.

She saw Lloyd's wagon bounce again. This time, just as the wheels came down there was another ridge, or maybe a shallow ditch. Whatever it was, she saw the rear wheel fold in on itself and the back end of the wagon dropped towards the ground. Lloyd tumbled backwards towards the rear of the wagon, and Jethro, not knowing what had happened tried to steer the horse to the right, to correct the movement. The wagon tail caught on the earth and suddenly Lloyd was on the ground, the two slave girls were flung into the air and the horse came to a halt, unable to drag the weight of the wagon, now on its side, forward.

'My God,' Plymouth said. He heaved his horse up, pulling his wagon alongside the wreckage.

Mary Colton jumped down, ran towards the girls, looking over her shoulder at the riders in the distance. There was blood streaming from a cut on Josephine's cheek, just below her eyes. Louvain was shaking, trying to stand, reaching out towards Josephine, tears rolling down her face.

Lloyd stood up, the shotgun in his hand.

'Behind the wagons,' he said.

Mary Colton glanced backwards again. Three of the riders were maybe 800 yards away. They were slowing now. She could clearly see one of them working the action on his rifle. The two that had gone wide were coming back towards them. One of them had only one arm.

'What gun have you got, Plym?' Lloyd said.

'I don't.'

'Goddamn. What are you doing — '

'I gave it to Buzzard.'

'I have a gun,' Mary said.

Lloyd looked at her and saw the tiny weapon in her hand.

'Jesus,' he said.

Jethro said, 'They don't know we ain't armed.'

'No,' Lloyd said. 'That's going to delay them by all of about . . . ten seconds.'

Mary looked again. The men were closing together again. Maybe 600 yards away now. Coming forward slowly. She saw one of them raise a rifle.

'Down!' she said.

And then a bullet smacked into the back of Lloyd's wagon at about the same moment that she heard the gunshot itself.

★ ★ ★

John Cowmeadow said, 'Jesus Christ.'

He was standing alongside his horse in the river shallows. The horse was drinking thirstily. John had splashed water over his own face and was drinking from his cupped hands when he heard the shot.

Raul scurried back up to the top of the bank. In winter the water might be raging all the way up there. Now they'd had to scrabble down the dirt to get the horses to the water. Nevertheless, a few yards out and the river was running fast and deep.

Another shot echoed out of the dawn.

'It's coming from across the river,' Washington said.

'You can't tell down here,' John said. 'They should be coming up the Romego trail on this side.'

'If it's them.'

'Yeah, if it's them,' John said. But who else would it be? It had seemed too easy. Follow a line from where Buzzard Jones had led them back in a north-easterly direction. Meet up with Plymouth King and the slaves and see them safely up to Romego. But who was to say that some folks back in Missouri hadn't seen what was going on and had decided to get a posse together?

'Can't see nothing,' Raul yelled. 'But it's definitely coming from the south.'

'Jesus,' John Cowmeadow said. 'Come on. Get the horses back out the water and let's go.'

He led his horse out of the river, heaved himself up, and urged her back up the steep bank.

A third shot echoed out.

'Speed it up!' Cowmeadow said. He looked at Washington and Isaiah, his other freed slave. 'I think we might have to save some more of your fellows.'

* * *

When the riders were 200 yards away and still approaching slowly, one of them raised his rifle, paused, and then shot Plymouth's horse in the neck. The horse collapsed without a sound. One moment it had been standing there, breathing heavily, waiting more instruction from its masters. Then its legs simply folded up beneath it and it went silently to the ground.

They came closer.

At 150 yards they shot Lloyd's horse. Lloyd's horse shrieked once and cried quietly as it died.

At eighty yards they stopped and one of them yelled, 'There ain't nothing and nobody in twenty miles. You're in Missouri and that means you abide by Missouri law.'

Another one of them laughed at that.

'You come any closer and we'll shoot,' Lloyd said.

They all laughed this time. And came closer.

At twenty yards Mary could see the dust coating their stubbled faces and dirtying their clothes. Their horses were sweating and one of them was rolling its head and stamping a foot.

'You have a choice,' one of them said. He was wearing a black vest, buttoned up over a blue shirt. 'You can die — I mean, you Kansas folk. You can die and then we take the slaves back. Or you can hand 'em over and we'll leave you be. It might be a long walk but you'll make it. There's plenty of water hereabouts.'

They were crouched down behind the splintered wood of Lloyd's wagon. There was barely even any illusion of protection. Plymouth had pulled his wagon alongside, but it made scarcely any difference. Mary could hear Louvain crying. She wondered just how bad life could be like back in the mines to create this much fear in the girl.

'They ain't slaves,' Lloyd said. 'They're free men and women. Same as you and me. They were kidnapped into slavery.'

'Tell it to the judge,' the man with one arm said. Mary studied his face. Yeah, little Frankie had been right. The man was good-looking. At least on the outside. Once you knew what sort of thoughts were going on inside his head he became uglier than an angry snake.

'We'll count to ten,' the man in the vest said. 'We get to ten, you either send the slaves out or we start shooting.'

He started counting. By the time he got to five there wasn't a single one of them who didn't have a gun in his hand.

* * *

Cowmeadow and his men galloped along the riverbank, in and out of the thick trees, keeping to high ground, trying to see ahead of them and trying to see across the water.

'Where in the hell are they?' John said.

The sound of a gunshot could carry a long way on the still air. But not *that* far. The thought that whatever Luther had set up, that whoever he was planning to bring across might be about to be lost to them drove him on. He spurred his horse cruelly, hating himself for it, but hating the idea of losing the men whom Luther had died for even more. For a while over the last few days he thought they'd lost them, that Luther's terrible death had been in vain. Then it suddenly started to look good again. Not that anything could make up for what they did to Luther — but at least some legacy would mean *something*.

The next gunshot sounded nearer.

'That was no rifle,' Cowmeadow said. 'That was — '

'They're across the river, boss,' Washington said, as they burst out of a group of trees. For a second they had a clear line of sight across the water, and across the plain on the far side. 'They're shooting them down.'

★ ★ ★

'Ten,' the vested man said.

Lloyd stood up from behind the wagon, the shotgun raised. He was half a second too slow. One of the riders to the vested man's right fired his rifle. The bullet hit Lloyd in the throat just as he squeezed the shotgun trigger. He was already falling backwards. The shotgun blast went skywards.

Mary stifled a sob and scuttled across to Lloyd. Blood was bubbling from his mouth. His eyes were wide and staring at her.

'Lloyd! No!'

A blood bubble rose on his lips. When it burst she screamed. His eyes glazed over. There were no more bubbles.

The other women were both crying. Mary placed a hand on the back of Lloyd's skull and was lifting his head as if somehow that might make a difference. The amount of blood on the ground beneath him sickened her.

Jethro was looking at her. 'We should give ourselves up,' he said.

'It won't make any difference,' Plymouth said. 'It's too late.'

'He's dead,' Mary said quietly. It seemed too easy, too quick. One moment he'd been there, been alive, and then he was gone. Dead. So quickly. So easily. So thoughtlessly.

'Who's next?' one of the riders called.

Mary slipped her finger around the trigger of her tiny gun. It felt like a hundred years and 10,000 miles away that her father had given it to her, a symbol more than a genuine attempt to provide her with something that would genuinely offer protection. Though maybe she was interpreting events based on what she now knew. This moment, when surely she was about to die, was as far away from her life in the schoolroom as the schoolroom had been from her life back East. She looked down at Lloyd. There was a look of surprise on his face, she realized. A hole the size of a penny in his throat. That was it. A surprised expression and a small hole. Again, it seemed so easy to die. Moments flashed before her, the points in time when it could have all been so different. Coming West. Meeting Father Wiseman and joining his mission. Jumping up on Plymouth

King's wagon — lying to him to make him believe Buzzard had trusted her. Lloyd deciding to head west at exactly the same time as they had. There were a thousand others, too. If only Luther had told them what he was planning they could have all gone after Jethro and the girls together. Made a new plan. Yet, even as she heard the man who had shot Lloyd working the action on his gun again, she knew she would have still done it all the same again. Some things were bigger than individual people.

A bullet slammed into the base of Lloyd's wagon, punched through the wood and buried itself into the ground near Louvain's foot. She screamed. A splinter of wood embedded itself in Mary's cheek.

Another bullet smashed through the wood.

All of them were pressed as hard into the ground as they could be. Except Jethro. Jethro, she saw, was going through Lloyd's pockets. He had the shotgun in his hand. He was looking for shells, she realized.

That was the only thing that was stopping the riders walking right up and pressing the muzzles of their guns against our heads, Mary thought. They don't know we're as good as unarmed.

Another bullet came through the wood. This one ricocheted off the iron axle and spun upwards, glinting in the low sun.

She saw Jethro had found some shells in Lloyd's jacket pocket. He had the gun broken open, slipping the shell inside.

The next bullet caught Plymouth in the thigh. She heard him grunt and the spray of blood splattered her face.

She crawled to the right, reached her hand around the edge of the wagon base, squeezed the trigger of her tiny gun.

She felt the weak kick of the Derringer, heard the quiet pop of the minuscule weapon.

Waited for them to laugh.

★　★　★

Isaiah, high up on the west bank of the river, pulled his rifle from his scabbard, raised it to his shoulder and took careful aim at one of the men across the river, who was shooting into the base of the overturned wagon. They were laughing, taking turns in shooting. Shouting out at the people cowering behind the thin wooden base of the wagon.

He gently squeezed the trigger.

When they'd freed him, several months before, he'd never fired a rifle in his life. He'd soon discovered a natural ability. Whenever they were out riding the far reaches of the boss's ranch it was always he who'd shoot the rabbit or the squirrels or the white-tailed deer that would provide supper.

He couldn't remember the last time he'd missed.

The rifle butt kicked against his shoulder.

Across the river one of the men spun off his horse and landed motionless on the ground.

* ★ ★

Jethro lay flat on the ground and stuck the barrel of the shotgun through one of the new holes in the base of Lloyd's wagon. He pulled the trigger. The shot gun roared. Then he rolled backwards and broke the gun ready to reload it.

There was another rifle shot. This one sounded as though it was coming from further away.

Now more, these closer again, a salvo of bullets smashing into the wagon, splinters burying themselves into their faces and hands. Josephine cried out. Plymouth grunted again. Jethro was breathing rapidly.

Another salvo.

'They're . . . circling,' Plymouth said. It sounded to Mary as if he was having trouble speaking. 'They're moving . . . round to the — there's two of them on the ground. We . . . got . . . two of them!'

He looked over his shoulder. There was blood on his lips.

Mary stared at him in disbelief.

230

Maybe her tiny bullet had been guided by God. Could it be that she'd really killed someone? She thought back to holding up Buzzard with an empty gun. It was the first time she'd had even an inkling of the power — the strength — that a gun gave a person. Until that moment she'd have never imagined she would have enjoyed those feelings. And back at the crossing, shooting through the rope, feeling the kick of the gun. The *power*. And now this? Had she actually killed someone? She thought of that bubble of blood exploding over Lloyd's face. I hope so, she thought. I goddamned well hope so. Then she felt a bullet crease the side of her head, actually pass through her hair. Half an inch to the left and she'd be dead.

But she was alive.

A second later she realized that the bullet that had missed her had killed Josephine, who had been sheltering behind her.

She wanted to scream again.

What good God now?

'They've seen us, boss,' Isaiah said. 'They're putting the wagons between us.'

'We have to cross the river,' Cowmeadow said.

'It's too deep,' Washington said. 'The current's too — '

'Come on, man!'

One time, when Washington was first old enough to understand, he'd seen a man drowned for trying to escape across a river. The bossman had said that as he'd liked water so much they'd let him spend the entire rest of his life swimming. They'd tied a massive iron wheel to the man's back, so heavy he couldn't walk, and then they'd held a branding iron close to the man's wife's face and invited him to crawl into the river.

'Come on, fellows!' Cowmeadow yelled. 'Into the water. It's a goddamn order.'

Isaiah lined up one more shot with

his rifle. The men were out of sight now, retreating and circling out of sight, but at least another shot might keep their heads down.

He fired, and then followed Jacques and Raul and Washington and the boss into the wild water.

14

There was so much blood that Buzzard wondered how it could be that he was still alive. The way they'd tied him, looping the rope around his wrists and pulling him tight to the pommel had opened up the wound even more than it had been when Cowmeadow's man had pressed his rifle into it. With every movement of the horse he could feel the blood soaking his shirt and running down his arm. Soaking the rope. Making his wrist slick.

Slick and slippery.

He started to work his hand backwards and forwards in the rope. Each time he moved his hand it seemed that the rope slipped a little further over the heel of his thumb. He thought back to the night when he'd been tied and hooded — it felt like weeks ago, yet it had only been, when? Yesterday? He'd needed patience and determination then. And he'd need the same now.

The sun was visible over the horizon now.

'What we'll do,' Wiseman said, and Buzzard quickly had to stop moving his hand. Wiseman hadn't said anything for hours, 'is let you see how it's all turned out. Just so you know how foolish it was to get mixed up in all of this.'

'Then what?' Buzzard said.

'Then we'll shoot you.'

When Wiseman looked away Buzzard started working his hand again. He could feel the coarse rope rubbing his skin away. It was starting to hurt more than his shoulder.

He worked it harder.

They were riding into an area of thicker trees now. The rider called Slim was up ahead scouring the trail for tracks. The closer they got to the river the taller and thicker grew the vegetation. The ground was still dry and dusty, but there were large areas where coarse grass was starting to survive. The low sun, shining through the trees, started to warm Buzzard's body. He hadn't realized how much of the shivering he'd been doing had been down to the cold rather than the pain.

He could get the rope right up on to the knuckle at the base of the thumb now, but in the process had just about rubbed all the lubricating blood away. Instead there was raw flesh.

One more hard yank might do it.

He took a deep breath, pulled his hand back as hard as he could and the pain caused him to gasp out loud.

A gunshot rang out somewhere to the east.

* * *

'Check his hands,' Wiseman said. 'And tie his horse to the tree.'

The rider called Slim rode across to Buzzard.

There was another gunshot in the distance.

'Let's hope we don't all get shot,'

Slim said. 'It's going to be a hot day even in the shade. You could die of thirst out of here.' He leaned across and looked at the knots, grabbed hold of Buzzard's right hand and pulled it hard upwards. His hand, with the left one tied beneath it, moved less than an inch.

'It might be worth it,' Buzzard said. 'If I knew you all'd been shot.'

Slim smiled.

'Don't you worry none. There's five men already ahead of us. We'll be coming right back to say goodbye. I'm sure Scoop will want to have some fun with you.'

He climbed down from his horse, took the reins from Buzzard's horse and passed them over and under a low branch on a red cedar tree, forming a loose knot.

'He's done, boss,' Slim said, climbing back on to his horse.

He winked at Buzzard.

'Later, my friend.'

Wiseman rode over. 'None of this is

personal, you understand. This is
. . . well, it's bigger than us. Genesis,
you know?'

'Why don't you leave me a Bible,'
Buzzard said. 'By the time you get back
I might be on your side.'

'When we come back I'll read a few
words from the Bible. I promise you
that.'

Then Wiseman turned his horse, and
he and his two riders, started racing
towards the river, and the gunshots.

★   ★   ★

Jethro was dead. Plymouth saw the
bullet that killed him. The riders, no
longer leisurely sitting back, no longer
talking amongst themselves and lazily
placing shots into the base of the wagon
as they waited for Plymouth and Lloyd
and Mary to give up the slaves, had
suddenly turned and galloped off to the
right, circling behind the wagons,
shooting like crazy both into the
wagons and across towards the river.

For a moment Plymouth hadn't understood what was happening. He thought Mary's tiny gun had got lucky, or maybe Jethro's shotgun blast had forced a decision. Possibly the two things together had given their attackers the impression that the small group cowering beneath splintered wood had more firepower than they really did have.

But then he'd heard more shots, these sounding different. He'd heard someone yell and he'd heard a horse shriek. Close by.

After that the men started firing into them from a new angle. No longer playing. Simply wanting to kill.

Plymouth had found himself lying hard up against the rump of his horse. He'd been hit twice, maybe three times. He could feel blood coming from his leg and his arm. His stomach felt as if it had been kicked by a mule. Mary was lying face down on the floor between Lloyd's body and Josephine's. He knew she was alive because she had her right hand clenched into a fist and was banging it slowly up and down on the ground.

Then he saw Jethro rise up, the shotgun in his hand, and a bullet caught him in the face. He was knocked backwards six feet, landed draped over the body of Lloyd's horse, and didn't move.

It had all been in vain. They were all going to die out here.

Another gunshot. Another bullet buried itself deep in the horse's dead flesh just inches from Plymouth. He didn't know whether Louvain was still alive. Hell, she couldn't talk anyway. But then, what the hell did it matter? They had no chance in hell of getting out of this.

He stole a glance back at Jethro. When the man had been hit and flung backwards he'd dropped the shotgun. It was lying about a yard beyond any cover whatsoever. It might as well have been in a gun store back in South Bottom for the good that it could do him now.

Another bullet whistled above them. Then another.

He pressed up as hard as he could to the horseflesh, and with his left hand he reached backwards until he found Mary's clenched fist.

He held her hand.

★   ★   ★

John Cowmeadow could feel the current pulling his horse downstream. She was working hard to fight it, legs working as fast as possible. But she was tired, too tired. At one point her head went under and he felt himself being pitched forwards. He hauled up on the reins with one hand, the other trying desperately to hold his rifle out of the water, and a moment later her head burst from the water spraying water upwards, snorting foam from her nose. But she was being washed downstream rapidly. The bank looked steeper down there, too.

'Come on!' he called. 'You can do it!'

Her head went under again, and again he hauled her up. They were in the middle of the river now. No turning back. He could feel her legs working beneath him, moving like paddles in the water. But she seemed so slow, so heavy.

For a second he thought about sliding off. He was no swimmer, but if it meant she'd make it then it would be worth it. He'd simply hang on to the side of his saddle and make it with her. But all of a sudden he realized she'd found her rhythm. She'd stopped fighting the water and was almost floating now, her body moving forwards in small jerks, just like a boat, he thought, paddles pushing the water back. Her head was up now, her ears erect. She might actually be enjoying this, he thought, and then he felt the movement change as her hoofs found the bottom. Suddenly she was bursting up on to the bank, shaking her head, spraying the water off.

He raced her up the dirt slope and on

to the grassland where, maybe 200 yards away, he could see the men firing round after round into some broken wagons.

★ ★ ★

Buzzard's left hand, the one that felt skinned to the bone, was shaking so much it took him ten minutes to work the knot loose from his right and free himself from the pommel.

He climbed down from the horse, and then discovered that his legs wouldn't support him. It was almost like being drunk. He tried to stand and his legs simply folded away beneath him and he crashed to the floor. His horse looked round at him.

'It ain't my fault,' he said. 'It's been a tough day.'

He used first the stirrup and then the saddle to heave himself upright. The sky felt as though it was rotating round his head. Everything went hazy and blurred. He found a canteen of water in a saddle-bag and took a long drink. His horse whinnied. He poured some of the water into his hat and held it out for her.

Then he untied her, and somehow he managed to clamber on to her back once more.

Again the sky seemed to spin, trails of blue and red and the last darkness of night pressing in on his brain. The darkness seemed to grow, almost as if dawn had decided to retreat this day.

Then total blackness came upon him.

When he next opened his eyes he was lying on the ground beside the horse, his right shoulder hurting now.

He lay still for several minutes. 'I can't do this,' he said. He wasn't sure whether he meant stand up, climb on to his horse, even stay on his horse. Let alone react to the sound of gunshots.

If there were gunshots.

Why would there be gunshots out here?

Why had they left him tied out here anyway?

The answers all seemed to be just out of reach and getting further away. The darkness was circling him again.

A dead man's boots. He wasn't sure if he said the words aloud or not. A dead man's . . . no, a *dying* man's boots. That was how it had started. If he'd cut back across the high ground instead of taking the easy route through Willow Canyon then the world would have been different. He wouldn't have found Luther Curry. Wouldn't have tried to make a quick buck by stealing his shoes and would never have found out that there was a whole world of evilness out there that even the Mexicans couldn't compete with. They'd almost killed him out there last night — no, the night before — when they'd hooded and beaten him. Maybe they had left him for dead. He'd had courage and tenacity then. But it was driven by indignation. But indignation gets beaten out of a man, he thought. Determination can only take you so far. They'd shot him. Had they been aiming for his shoulder or his heart? He thought of Luther's hollow eye sockets again and that made him think of Scoop. Then there was Blue. The man with a wife and daughter across the river whom he hadn't seen in a year and never would now. Hell, the wife and daughter didn't even know Blue was dead. It was so quick. So easy. And elsewhere it would last for ever.

He realized he was shaking his head. The pain took it out of a man. It stripped the life from him as surely as it stripped the skin and the flesh and the . . . eyes. Being beaten and shot and then riding all night. Being tied in an agonizing position and feeling the blood run out of you, leaving you weak and dizzy and unable to stand. Like a new-born horse. Like a drunkard. He thought of Molloy's saloon. What wouldn't he give for one of Molloy's beers and a whiskey chaser right now?

He lifted the reins. The leather felt heavy. His arms felt weak. Now the warming sun was no longer making him feel good, instead it was making him feel nauseated.

'I can't do it,' he said aloud. 'I'm just Buzzard Jones, thief. I should go back to picking the bones of the dead.'

★　★　★

When the only thing Plymouth could hear was Mary's harsh breathing, the sound of Louvain crying, and the whistle of his own breath; when the sound of gunfire was nothing more than an echo inside his head that rebounded around and around as if it would never die, when the sound and the vibration of riders racing across the earth was gone, he tried to stand.

His leg screamed at him. His belly felt as if it would tear open. He held on to the splintered wood of the wagon and inch by inch worked his way upright.

Everything was unreal. It was like living in a nightmare brought on by too much time spent around the dead. The low sun on the grass, casting huge shadows from even the smallest bushes and rocks, had a clarity to it that felt new — and thus strange. The smell of the river water in the air was stronger and clearer. The whisper of a breeze on his cheek caressed him with a softness of touch that he couldn't recall having felt before. The sound of sobbing, of laboured breathing, of his own heartbeat and the blood it pushed around his body, was loud and distinct.

He adjusted his spectacles. There was nobody in sight. Where the men who had slaughtered them had been the land was empty.

He understood little of it. Who the men were — either group of men. But did it matter? He turned. Mary was looking up at him. There was blood around her mouth and he felt a hollow feeling inside. Had she been gutshot?

'Have they gone?' she said. Her voice was even, too even. It sounded almost dead.

He nodded. But as he spoke he

imagined he could hear more distant gunfire.

'Are you . . . How bad is it?'

'I don't know,' she said. She held out her hand and he helped her up, his own pain forgotten for a moment.

'Louvain?' he said.

The slave girl was curled up in a ball, her hands over her head. They could see her back rising and falling.

Mary turned gingerly. Slowly and carefully she crouched down by the girl, put her hand on Louvain's shoulders, told her it was OK, that it was all over.

After maybe thirty seconds the girl dropped her hands. She pounded the ground softly several times. Another minute and she raised her head. Her face wet from tears, dirty from the grass and dust. She reached out and hugged Mary Colton and they stayed that way for maybe five minutes.

Then Plymouth felt the first vibrations of movement through the ground. Still holding on to the wrecked wagon he turned, saw nothing, turned again.

And there, coming out of the trees by the river were three more riders, their horses dripping river water.

He thought he recognized the one in front, but his vision was blurred. He didn't know whether it was too much blood on his face or too little of it in his veins.

'Someone coming,' he said.

Mary looked round.

'Thank God,' she said. 'It's Father Wiseman.'

15

Later, Plymouth King knew he should have worked it out. What the hell was Wiseman doing out here? He must have followed someone — and if he was following someone then he was involved. *Properly* involved. But right then the pain and the dizziness and the fact that he could just stand back, relax, close his eyes, and let someone else take over, was enough.

Wiseman and his two riders rode up towards them.

'Plymouth King,' Wiseman said. 'What on earth . . . ?'

Plymouth said, 'Father . . . '

'What happened?'

Plymouth shook his head. 'I don't know. We were followed. They . . . ' He looked down at the bodies of his friends tangled up behind the wagons. 'Lloyd,' he said, but couldn't find any more words.

'They killed Lloyd,' Mary said, stifling a sob.

Wiseman glanced back at his partners. One of them was looking out across the plain to hills and trees in the distance. 'There's some horses yonder,' he said.

'And bodies on the ground,' another said.

'Check them out,' Wiseman said. He didn't sound happy. 'Did you see them? Who were they?'

Plymouth said. 'I didn't see them.'

'Someone from the territory,' Mary said. 'I recognized one of them.'

'You recognized one of them?'

'He had an arm missing.'

'Where did they go?' Wiseman said.

'Someone else came,' Plymouth said. 'Chased them off. There was shooting.'

'Someone else, huh? It's a regular crossroads,' Wiseman said. 'Who were *they*?'

Mary looked at him. The way he was speaking, this wasn't the Father Wiseman she knew. There was something different about him. He showed no interest in Lloyd's body, no interest in Jethro or Josephine. No interest in their injuries.

'We didn't see,' she said.

'There was a lot of shooting,' Plymouth said. '*Too much* shooting.'

'If you . . . ' Wiseman shook his head. There were red patches flaring in his cheeks.

'What is it, Father?' Mary said.

'Boss,' one of the riders said; he'd ridden out in a loop to where the bodies of two men lay. The dead men's horses had retreated several hundred yards and were now watching the group nervously.

'What is it, Slim?'

'It's Johnson and Kirby. They're both dead.'

Wiseman used language that Mary never expected to hear from a priest.

'Father . . . '

'You know these people?' Plymouth said. 'The ones — '

'Shut up! Yeah, I know them. Kirby's

the one — was the one — with just one arm,' Wiseman said. 'They were good men.'

'They were trying to kill us!' Mary said.

'If you hadn't been so . . . interfering. Damn it! You . . . your type make me sick.'

'Father!'

'I tried to talk you out of it,' he said. 'I tried to warn you.' His horse snorted and whinnied. Wiseman pulled her round in a tight circle.

'Who killed my men?' he said, the anger hotter now. 'Who killed my men?'

The words hit Mary like the bullet that had buried itself in her arm. Father Wisemen didn't just know the men who had been shooting at them, they were *his men*. The men who had trailed them from South Bottom. The man with one arm who'd given her the original note about Luther Curry. *His men*. She actually felt her knees weaken.

'Your men?' Plymouth said.

'Who killed them?' Wiseman yelled. As he spoke he swung a punch at Plymouth and knocked him to the ground.

Mary screamed. 'You!' she said, fumbling beneath her skirt for something. Louvain was standing right behind her, like a child sheltering behind its mother's skirt. Mary found she was leaning on the girl for support.

'Search them, Slim,' Wiseman said to one of his men. 'Make sure they don't have any guns.'

'It was you!' Mary said, looking at Wiseman.

Slim dismounted, and roughly ran his hands over her.

'Get off me!'

'I'll shoot you,' he said quietly, 'as soon as look at you. You killed some very good men. Better than you'll ever be.'

'It wasn't us. It was — '

'Who? Who was it?' Wiseman roared.

Slim had his hands inside Mary's skirt. She struggled and he slapped her.

Tears sprung into her eyes. Not through pain, but because of the injustice . . . no, the betrayal.

Slim found the Derringer.

'She had a baby gun, boss,' he said.

'She got bullets?'

Slim held up the pouch.

'She can see how it feel to lose a man. Load the gun. Let's see how she likes to see a friend die.'

'You . . . bastard,' Mary said.

Wiseman smiled, but his breath was coming in fast snorts as if he was a bull about to charge.

'You sent these men,' Mary said. 'Luther said there was a . . . How could you? After all you said? After all you've done?'

Wiseman sighed.

'I wish I had time to explain. But — '

'I don't believe this,' Plymouth said. 'You said prayers over Luther's grave.'

'I'm still a priest. I meant what I said.'

Mary spat at him.

'You're evil!'

'Well, well. The girl has a bit of spirit after all. I always took you for an Eastern girl just wanting to do something to tell your friends about at home.'

'I . . . I hope you rot in Hell.'

'Well, if I do, I'm going to be there quite some time after you. You killed two of my men. Two of my friends.'

'We didn't — '

'It was your meddling!' Wiseman roared. 'Who's the girl?'

'You don't know?' Mary said.

'I can guess *who* she is. What's her name?'

'Louvain.'

'Good. See those trees down by the river. We're going to go and have some fun. You understand?'

Mary felt a sickness rising within her.

'What do you mean?' Plymouth said.

'My buddy, here. We call him Scoop. You want to know why?'

No one said anything.

'See, he likes to scoop people's eyes out.'

'Luther . . . ' Plymouth said.

'Yeah, he had a bit of fun with Luther. He's lost a couple of good friends. He deserves his fun.'

'What are you going to do?' Plymouth said.

'Well, for starters we'll tie young quiet Louvain here to — '

'She can't talk,' Mary said. 'That's why she's quiet.'

'Good for her. She won't be able to see, soon.'

'Please,' Plymouth said. 'There's no need — '

'You're right,' Wiseman said. 'There is no need. But you see, you killed — '

'We didn't kill them!' Mary cried.

'What we'll do,' Wiseman said, 'is see how much pain Louvain here can endure before Mary decides she's willing to shoot you, Plymouth.'

★ ★ ★

Louvain sounded like an animal when she screamed. Plymouth grabbed hold of Slim and tried to pull him off her. Slim let the girl go, turned and, in the same movement, punched Plymouth in the face. Plymouth stumbled backwards and fell.

Wiseman laughed.

'Come on, get them over to the trees.'

Slim carried on hauling Louvain towards the river.

Then Scoop said, 'There's some folks coming, boss. Over yonder.'

Everyone turned. There were three riders coming across the plain, from the direction where the unknown group had chased Wiseman's riders.

'Who is it?' Slim asked.

Wiseman said, 'I recognize that man's shape anywhere. That's John Cowmeadow.'

Plymouth, still on the ground, felt a moment of hope flare in his heart. But then he saw Wiseman's face. Just for a moment, the way the low sun cast shadows from his brows and nose and lips it looked like a skull rather than a face on his shoulders.

'He'll get real close,' Wiseman said.

'Wait until he starts to talk and then kill them all.'

Plymouth saw that there was blood on John Cowmeadow's face. One of his men had been shot in the elbow and blood was soaking through his jacket. He was whistling with pain as he breathed. Another of his men was a black man. So what Mary had said had been true. Cowmeadow was one of the good ones.

'Looks like you been in a fight,' Wiseman said as Cowmeadow pulled his horse to a halt.

John Cowmeadow said, 'Father Wiseman. What brings you . . . ?'

Cowmeadow's voice died. Plymouth could almost see the understanding appear in the man's eyes.

'You,' he said.

'Where's the rest of my men,' Wiseman said.

'Dead,' John Cowmeadow said and went for his gun.

Slim, standing there with his left hand still clutching Louvain's wrist and a revolver already in his right hand but turned side on to Cowmeadow so that the big man couldn't see the gun, shot John Cowmeadow in the chest. John Cowmeadow went backwards off the horse.

One of the others, not the black man, was trying to get a gun from his holster. It was caught on something. Slim turned, had time to shake his head, and he shot that man too.

The last of Cowmeadow's men, the black man, turned towards Slim, trying to bring his rifle down. He hesitated just a moment as his eyes lit upon Father Wiseman. In that moment of hesitation Scoop shot him, the bullet taking the man's jaw off. He was still sitting on horse, his eyes wide with surprise and shock, when Slim shot him in the chest.

'Just to make sure,' Slim said.

Wiseman looked at Plymouth and then at Mary.

'You kill my friends,' he said. 'You die.'

They put one bullet in the Derringer

and told Mary to shoot Plymouth King.

'You'll need to place the barrel right against his head,' Slim said. 'On account of that itsy bitsy bullet won't make it more than about six inches.'

Louvain was tied to a tree.

Scoop had started a fire with dry dead wood and kindling from the trees and was heating a strip of iron they'd broken off Lloyd Avery's wagon. They'd yanked Louvain's dress down past her shoulders.

'See how long you can bear it,' Wiseman said to Mary, 'Before putting her out of her misery by shooting Plymouth.'

'Fun, ain't it?' Scoop said, pressing the iron against Louvain's shoulder, hearing the flesh sizzle and smelling the burning, hearing that animal scream again, watching the tears roll down her cheek, listening to Mary's foul language and hearing Plymouth say, 'Do it, Mary. Do it, Mary.'

'Wait until we get to the eyes,' Wiseman said.

★ ★ ★

There were two moons. It reminded him of a time some months before. Was it months? It felt like for ever. And there they were again. Two of them. No, now they were coalescing. That was a word he'd used before, wasn't it? Back then before . . . before what? He heard some shooting. He'd heard a lot of shooting. He assumed that these were just echoes of that earlier shooting. It was nothing to worry about. Just an echo in the darkness.

His horse plodded on southwards, the river to its left. He wasn't really sure where he was going. Sometime, somehow he knew he'd make it home. He'd see all his friends again. Plymouth . . . wasn't Plymouth going to do something for him? And Mary Colton. He was looking forward to seeing Mary again. She was pretty. He smiled to himself. He might ask her . . . ask her what? He couldn't remember what it was he wanted to ask her.

Both shoulders were hurting. His hand was on fire. His belly felt as if he'd been kicked by a horse, knifed by an Indian, and bitten by a snake.

He pulled his water skin from his saddle, lifted it to his mouth. It was empty.

A dizziness came over him and he had to lean forward over the horse's neck to stay on board.

'Whoah,' he said. 'Not good. Let's go to the river.'

Then he heard some screaming. It sounded like an animal. It sounded human. And it sounded like nothing he'd ever heard before.

So he knew it couldn't be an echo inside his head.

★ ★ ★

At the river his horse drank thirstily. He sat on her back, leaning backwards for balance, and looked longingly down at the water. It looked cool and refreshing. He could taste it even whilst sat high on the horse. But he knew that if he got down he wouldn't be able to get back on her back again. No, it was safer just to sit here and . . .

There was that animal scream again. He turned his head.

What was it?

There it was again. He twisted further in his saddle, trying to pinpoint where the sound was coming from. His horse lifted her head. Suddenly his balance was wrong. He tried to adjust, reached out with his hand for the reins, but the leather and raw skin made him gasp in pain. Then he was falling, sliding off the side of the horse.

'Not again,' he said, and hit the water.

He came up spluttering for breath, the water running off his hair, down his face, cooling him, almost immediately easing the pain. He knelt in the water for a few minutes. He reached down and cupped his hands, filled them with water, drank thirstily, again and again. His horse was looking at him again.

'What?' he said.

And heard another scream.

It was a girl. How had he not realized that before?

He stood up, clothes pasted to him with freezing water.

'Where are they?' he said aloud, not wanting to hear the girl's terrible scream again, but needing to know where she was.

The silence seemed to last for ever. Nothing but the sound of the river, birds, wind in the trees, his horse breathing heavily and drinking.

And sometime, after a long break, another scream.

It came from across the river.

He mounted the horse, easily now. 'Can you swim?' he said, and heeled her into the river.

★ ★ ★

He came out of the trees on the Missouri side. The light seemed brighter here. He was staring into the

266

rising sun. The grasslands stretched towards distant hills, there were more trees to the south. He saw several horses down there, not wild, but saddled. Just standing there looking up at him, maybe fifty yards away. Then his eyes adjusted to the low sunlight and in front of him he could see the flattened grass where wagons and horses had recently passed. He looked to his left, and several hundred yards away he could make out what he thought was a pair of wagons, parked haphazardly.

Staying close to the trees he worked his way towards the wagons.

The next scream was louder, closer. He felt his heart begin to race. Somehow he knew that he was going to find Wiseman up here. Wiseman and the man called Scoop. It was going to end as it had started and he wasn't sure he had the courage to come face to face with more of Scoop's work.

He shuddered, and couldn't decide whether it was fear or his soaking clothes.

'Stay here,' he whispered to his horse, and climbed down to the ground.

He crouched as he moved, remembering something he'd been told when preparing to ambush the Mexicans. *Keep your head down. If they can't see you they can't shoot you.* He moved from tree to tree and just at the point where he started to hear men's voices — one laughing, one pleading, and one urging someone to shoot the old man — he saw the bodies over by the wagons.

He leant against a tree, wiped the water from his face, and listened, trying to gauge where the men were.

Now he heard someone, a woman, crying, begging for them to stop. And something else, too, a smell . . . the smell of a branding-iron. His stomach churned. He thought of Luther. He thought of Scoop.

And he realized that he had no weapon.

When the girl screamed again he ran for the bodies, head down, crouched as low as he could, the pain in his body forgotten now, washed away by cold water and hot fear. At the wagons he knelt down. Jesus. He wasn't sure but he thought this was Plymouth's wagon. The tongue was still attached to Plym's horse. His dead horse. He worked his way along the far side of the wagons, trying to keep out of sight if anyone was looking across from the river. My God, he said. There was Lloyd Avery, the man who ran the *Sentinel*. Next to him a thin man, whose face looked devoid of flesh. A woman too. All dead.

There'd been a massacre here, he thought.

He worked his way back along the cover of the wagons. Several more bodies lay out in the open. Keeping low, he ran across to them.

It was John Cowmeadow. And there, one of John's black riders, and there was the Mexican who had first spotted Buzzard's horse yesterday, hiding out in the hollow by the dry riverbank. It felt like a hundred years ago.

A sadness and an anger swept over him. He'd only known John Cowmeadow a few days, and for most of that time they'd either been fighting or Cowmeadow had been intent on killing him. But now, looking down at the man's body he felt a despair rising up. They'd finally come to understand one another. And now Cowmeadow was dead. His men, too.

There was a gun in John Cowmeadow's hand.

Buzzard Jones eased the dead man's fingers from around the handle, checked to see how many bullets were in there, and then looked back towards the river. He could see a line of flattened grass where whoever it was — Wiseman and his men, he guessed — had dragged their captives towards the river, towards the trees.

Who were those captives, he wondered? He figured one was Plymouth. But who was the woman?

He worked his way low and fast back into the trees along the river. Now he was extra careful, thinking back to the ambush all those years ago. *Silence means silence,* their captain had said. *When you're up in those rocks you don't even breathe.*

The smell of fire came to him. The crackle of burning sticks. The moaning of a woman in pain, and a man saying, 'We've almost got it red hot again. We'll just burn the other one, and then maybe we'll start on her face. That is unless you want to shoot your friend Plymouth, young lady.'

And there they were. Wiseman and Scoop. A girl he'd never seen before tied to a tree, the front of her skirt ripped open, long thin burn marks on her shoulders and her chest. Her head was hanging down but she was still conscious. Buzzard could hear her making strange moaning sounds. And tied to a tree along side her, Plymouth King, his face bloodied, dark stains on his jacket and trousers, yet his spectacles still on, albeit pushed up on his forehead, and some defiance still in his

271

eyes. He was looking at a woman who had her back to Buzzard.

'Next time, shoot me,' he said. 'Maybe they'll end it quickly then.'

Wiseman laughed.

'No they won't,' the woman said, and turned to look at the one called Scoop. He was holding an iron bar in the fire.

Buzzard had to stifle a gasp.

It was Mary Colton, looking as bloodied and beaten as Plymouth.

Buzzard took a deep breath, raised the gun he'd prised from John Cowmeadow's hand, and was just about to step into the clearing when he felt something hard and cold press against the back of his neck.

'Buzzard Jones, I believe,' the rider called Slim said.

★ ★ ★

Wiseman said, 'Well, well. I was thinking of you, Buzzard. The last loose end. Figured you were out there bleeding to death.'

Slim pushed Buzzard into the clearing, towards the fire. He had the gun that Buzzard had taken off John Cowmeadow in his left hand and his own Colt in his right.

Plymouth said, 'Buzzard. My God, how did you get here?'

Mary Colton looked at him, her lips trembled, she glanced briefly at Wiseman and then took two stumbling steps towards Buzzard and flung her hands around his neck.

She swore afterwards that she never meant to pull the trigger on the tiny Derringer, that there had honestly been no plan. Wiseman and his men had convinced her that the only way such a tiny gun could kill was if she placed it right against someone's temple — or preferably eye — and pulled the trigger. That was what they'd had her do with Plymouth whilst they tortured Louvain — press the gun against his eye, insist she put the slave girl out of her agony by killing a friend.

She said that it had been an accident,

that she must have caught her finger on Buzzard's collar.

She said that the bullet could just as easily have gone into Buzzard's neck.

What happened was: the moment she clasped her hands around his neck he heard the pop of the gun being discharged and he heard Slim grunt in pain and fall to the floor.

Buzzard, still with Mary holding him tight, looked down at Slim. The man wasn't moving. For a second Buzzard couldn't fathom what had happened. Then he noticed Slim's right eye — or where Slim's right eye should have been — was just a black hole.

Then Scoop reacted.

Buzzard heard the movement and turned. Scoop was rising up from beside the fire, holding the red-hot iron strip like a sword in front of him.

Wiseman, too, was moving. Fumbling to pull a revolver from his jacket pocket.

Buzzard threw Mary backwards, away from the iron, on to the ground. Then he dived towards Slim, reaching out for a gun, either gun, John Cowmeadow's or Slim's own.

He got his hand on the revolver, slipped his fingers around the grip, just started to lift it up, feeling the good weight in his hand, when Scoop laid the red hot iron across his wrist.

Buzzard screamed, and though he tried to hold on to the gun, the pain was too much. His flesh sizzled and smoke rose up from his flesh. He rolled away from Scoop, his peripheral vision picking up the glint of sunlight on the barrel of the gun that Slim had been holding in his other hand.

He grabbed the gun as he rolled. But Scoop stayed with him, aiming for Buzzard's face with the hot iron now, catching Buzzard's cheek and hair. Buzzard scrabbled away from him, his feet kicking at Slim's body.

'Out the way, Scoop,' Wiseman said; he had his own revolver held out in front of him now.

Scoop threw the hot iron at Buzzard's face and stepped swiftly aside.

Buzzard jerked his head back out of the way of the iron and then tried to get his right arm, the arm holding the gun, out from under him.

'Too slow,' Wiseman said.

Mary Coltman flung herself at Wiseman a second before he started firing. She raked his face with her fingernails, tried to get to his eyes. He was firing the gun. She had no idea where the bullets were going. She felt his flesh tear beneath her hands. He yelled, forced a hand against her face and sent her sprawling towards the fire.

Buzzard was sitting upright, his gun raised.

Scoop was lying face down, the back of his head a bloody pulp.

'You killed your own man, Father,' he said, and shot Father Wiseman in the chest.

16

They untied Plymouth and Louvain. They carried Louvain down to the river and bathed her burns in the cool water. Mary insisted that Buzzard took care of his burns, too. They dressed Plymouth's wounds best they could. Afterwards they enticed the loose horses back up to the wagons, and hitched one of them to Plymouth's flatbed. They laid John Cowmeadow and Lloyd Avery, the white slave called Jethro and Louvain's sister Josephine in the back of the wagon. There was no room for the others, the black man whom John Cowmeadow had employed, the Mexican who had first spied Buzzard's horse hidden away. Buzzard thought now, if they hadn't spotted him, if Raul hadn't glanced to his left at just that moment then everything would have been different. I wouldn't be here, Buzzard thought. I'd have been on the way back to town, or to Herb's. Either way, what had been going on here — with the fire and the iron and Scoop — would have gone on and on until its ultimate conclusion.

'I hate to leave them,' Plymouth said.

'We can come back,' Buzzard said, but both he and Plymouth knew that they wouldn't.

'We should at least bury them,' Mary said.

Buzzard nodded, but Plymouth said, 'We should. But we've not got spades or picks.'

Buzzard climbed up on to his own horse. Mary took one of the loose horses. They set off north, towards the shallows at Black Rock.

Plymouth looked back over his shoulders at the wreckage of Lloyd's wagon, the place where he'd come as close to dying as at any other time in his life. He looked at the bodies they were abandoning.

Buzzard said, 'You hate to leave

them, don't you?'

'Uh-huh.' Then he forced a smile. 'You?'

Buzzard smiled back. 'There was a time,' he said, 'when I'd be looking at their boots and coats and guns.'

'But?'

'My days of bone-picking are done, Plym. I'm happy leaving the dead behind.'

Epilogue

Louvain was eventually passed into the hands of the man called Powder, in Romego, on 8 July 1855. From there she went through several more stations on the underground before ultimately ending up in Washington where she testified before the Senate on the reality of slavery — both black and white — in Missouri. As she was unable to talk, it was through careful interrogation and — as was discovered — Louvain's amazing ability to draw that her evidence was given. Her pencil and charcoal sketches told the stories of what had happened and were so chilling that they could never be published. But to this day they reside in the vaults below Congress.

Back in New Whitby Buzzard Jones, whom few people knew could write, took over Lloyd Avery's *Sentinel*. He told the story of Jethro, Josephine and Louvain, although he never mentioned Father Wiseman. He wrote movingly of the plight of slaves — including white slaves — in his *Sentinel*. He networked his stories through other Kansas newspapers too, and slowly but surely the tide of opinion changed. In January 1861 Kansas joined the Union as a free state.

Just months later, the Civil War that would ultimately see the end of widespread slavery in America, commenced.

Plymouth King expanded his funeral business throughout western Kansas and married a girl called Edith who had joined him as a secretary. They had a son, whom they named Luther.

New Whitby puzzled for years on where their wonderful priest, Father Wiseman, had disappeared to. Eventually a young Irish lad called Gordon turned up and took over the church duties. The town felt complete again.

Buzzard Jones married Mary Colton

on 1 June 1856. It was a passionate and perfect summer and the horrors of the previous year faded. They made a part-investment in a new hotel. Mary continued teaching. Few people remembered the old Buzzard, the one they'd called a bone-picker and a thief.

In 1861, when the war came, Buzzard, already an experienced soldier, joined the Third Kansas Volunteers alongside his old comrade Herb Jordan.

'We need to finish what we started,' he told a tearful Mary. She had been waiting for the perfect moment to tell him that she was pregnant. The moment never came.

He asked Plymouth King to look after her.

Just about the whole town lined the streets and waved Buzzard off to war.

In August of that year he marched on Wilson's Creek. It was a bloody battle and Buzzard took a musket ball in the right knee. It was the end of his war. He was carried off the battlefield, and had his wound dressed in a field hospital. Three months later, walking as well as he ever would again, he limped and rode back across western Missouri and into Kansas.

In New Whitby, on a Tuesday, he tied his horse to the rail outside the school house, waited outside the door for a moment, listening. It wasn't Mary taking the lesson. He eased open the door, puzzled. Twelve children, boys and girls, turned and stared at him. The girl at the head of the class said, 'Yes? Can I help you, sir?'

Buzzard said, 'Mary? I was looking for Mary Colton.'

The girl smiled. 'I'm teaching her class for the time being.'

'Is she . . . is she all right?'

'Oh yes. She's fine. You are?'

'I'm Buzzard . . . I mean, Sam. Sam Jones, her husband.'

One of the girls in the back row giggled.

'Sam Jones,' the girl said, walking between the desks. 'She talks about you every day.' She held out her hand. 'Caroline Wallon. I'm honoured, Mr Jones.'

'You are?'

'Lots of people talk about you, Mr Jones.'

'They do?'

More laughter from the children.

'Please, where is Mary. I thought . . .'

'She'll be at home. Across the street. The hotel.' She said it as if she thought he was crazy for not having already been there.

'I'll . . . I'll try there. Thank you.'

He turned, not sure why he felt so self-conscious. Maybe it was all those children staring and smiling and laughing.

Halfway across the street he could still hear their laughing. He looked back. They had all come out of the schoolhouse and were standing on the plankwalk, looking over at him.

He turned again, and saw the main door of the hotel opening, Mary standing there, as beautiful as on that first day that she'd slipped a hand through his arm, walked him down the road and told him off for not taking a side in the fight against slavery.

She stared at him.

He stared back.

There was a child, a baby in her arms, wrapped in a blue blanket. Now she was smiling, crying, holding the baby out towards him and he was running, stumbling, cursing his ruined leg, and behind him he could hear all her schoolchildren cheering and clapping. Then he was there, holding her, holding them, staring down at the baby. His baby. His woman. His home.

His Kansas.

Other titles in the
Linford Western Library:

HELL FIRE IN PARADISE

Chuck Tyrell

Laurel Baker lost her husband and her two boys on the same day. Then, menacingly, logging magnate Robert Dunn rides into her ranch on Paradise Creek to buy her out. Laurel refuses as her loved ones are buried there — prompting Dunn to try shooting to get his way. Laurel's friends stick by her, but will their loyalty match Dunn's ten deadly gunmen? And in the final battle for her land, can she live through hell fire in Paradise?

THE BLACK MOUNTAIN DUTCHMAN

Steve Ritchie

In Wyoming, when Maggie Buckner is captured by a gang of outlaws, 'the Dutchman' is the only one who can free her. Near Savage Peak, the old man adjusts the sights on his Remington No. 1 rifle as the riders come into range. When he stops shooting, three of the captors lay dead. After striking the first deadly blows, the Dutchman trails the group across South Pass like the fourth horseman of the apocalypse . . . and surely Hell follows with him.